I0793466

10 YEAR ANNIVERSARY

Cofounders: Taj Forer and Michael Itkoff
Copy editor: Laura Fredrickson

© 2014 Daylight Community Arts Foundation

Photographs © 2013 Mike Osborne

All rights reserved

ISBN 978-0-9889831-4-4

Printed in China

No part of this publication may be reproduced, stored in a retrieval system, or transmitted in any form or by any means without the prior permission in writing of copyright holders and of the publisher.

Daylight Books

E-mail: info@daylightbooks.org

Web: www.daylightbooks.org

Cover image: Wendover Quadrangle Map (1972), courtesy of the U.S. Geological Survey

FLOATING ISLAND

MIKE OSBORNE

Daylight

Wendover Quadrangle Map (1972), courtesy of the U.S. Geological Survey

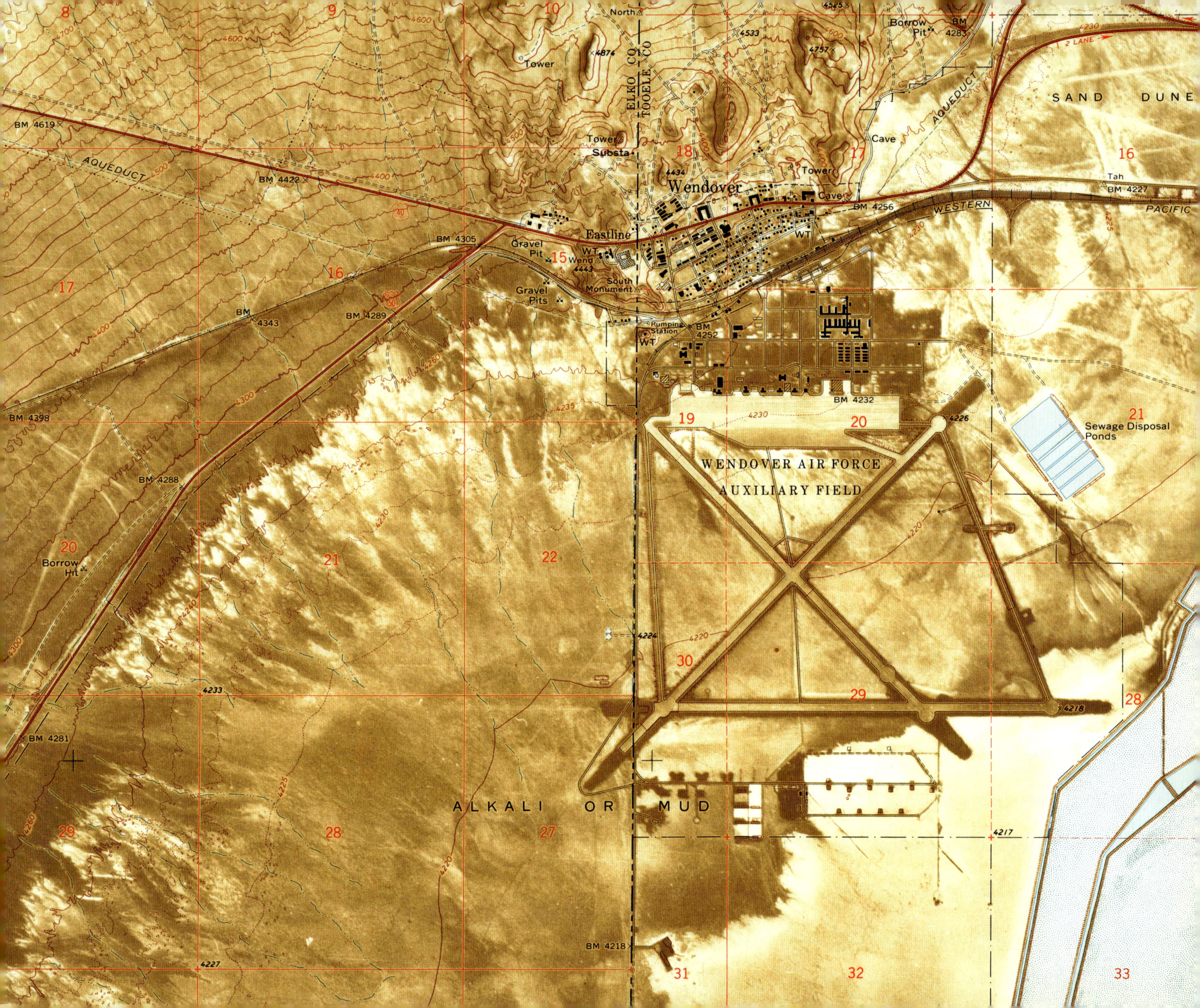

Wendover
Eastline
WENDOVER AIR FORCE
AUXILIARY FIELD
ELKO CO
TOOELE CO
AQUEDUCT
SAND DUNE
WESTERN
PACIFIC
Sewage Disposal
Ponds
ALKALI OR MUD
Tower
Substa
Cave
Borrow Pit
Gravel Pit
Gravel Pits
South Monument
Pumping Station
Borrow Ht
BM 4619
BM 4422
BM 4305
BM 4343
BM 4289
BM 4398
BM 4288
BM 4281
BM 4252
BM 4232
BM 4256
BM 4227
BM 4283
BM 4218

N 40° 43' 38.7", W 114° 2' 17.9"

The border runs north-south. To the west: Nevada; to the east: Utah. The town straddles the line. It is one town but also two towns. Wendover, in Utah, came first. When it spread across the border and into Nevada, the new town was called West Wendover. It was the same as the old town, but it had its own laws.

People arrived a century ago, though of course there had been others before them. The train brought them but hardly in droves. Twenty-five years later the Army Air Force came, drawn to nothingness and the freedom it offered.

Military personnel erected fences to delineate and own the emptiness. Entry was prohibited. On the range's perimeter, they built barracks and hangars, clinics and mess halls. They carved an immense X onto the land, a place to take off and touch down.

From the ground, they launched rockets with names like JB-2 Loon. The rockets arced over the desert floor while men watched through slits in concrete bunkers. From the air, they dropped Little Boy and Fat Man clones and measured their success. At night, the tachometric sight that predicted the bombs' trajectories was secured in a vault, like some object for a pharaoh's next life.

When the war was over, the troops no longer needed the town. They moved across the state to a bigger base. At Mach 1.0, the distance could be covered in ten minutes.

o

In the military's absence, there were not enough people to keep entropy at bay. Salt ate indiscriminately. Wood, metal, concrete—it didn't matter. Money became scarce, too.

There were things that could be done with the land. Extractive entities undertook the work, shaping the terrain with large machines. The firms' names—Intrepid, Vertellus—were enigmatic, evoking classified missions and distant planets.

Moviemakers appeared from time to time. The blankness of the landscape meant it could be anything. They used it to tell stories of catastrophe, invasion, and the afterlife. The pictures they made traveled far, so that when a visitor first encountered the place, it was with a strange sense of remembrance.

Mostly casinos filled the void created by the military's departure. They had been there all along, but they became something more. Historic names like Silver Smith, State Line, and Goldrush gave way to new names—Nugget, Rainbow, Montego Bay. After dark, the words radiated promise. Their light traveled across the desert for miles in search of a surface to describe.

The casinos called themselves resorts, and people resorted to them. Many came by car and truck and tour bus. On Fridays, the parking lots were full. They also arrived on daily planes that landed on the giant X. Shuttles waited by the tarmac to convey them onward.

The destinations were vast hotels tethered to cavernous halls with mirrored walls and ceilings that doubled their dimensions. Everything one could need was available within. In the hearts of the casinos, machines were lined up in rows. Their screens glowed, and they emitted the sounds of clinking coins and electronic arpeggios. The sounds proved the machines were working. Money was being made, life sustained.

o

Geological time is longer. Most of what is visible was once underwater, nearly a thousand feet of it. Fifteen thousand years ago, a Pleistocene lake stretched from the Wasatch Front to Idaho, where its excess overflowed with biblical violence before moving on to the Pacific. The peaks around Wendover broke the lake's surface and made small islands and archipelagos. When the water receded and exposed the mountains, it made a record of the process. It etched topographical lines in rock—a crude map inscribed on the land long before any place had a name.

What used to be the bottom of the lake extends out in a salty Cartesian plane. A land survey describes the surface as alkali or mud—a statement of fact as well as an admission of ambiguity and flux.

Twenty miles from the interstate, Floating Island rises out of the white expanse, its gray-brown rocks made blue by distance. Its profile is low and sleek, as if designed with velocity in mind. Light and heat make an inferior mirage. They turn the salt into a mirror that brings a sliver of sky down to the ground. The island hovers slightly above the horizon—a real illusion.

I. FLOATING ISLAND

1.1

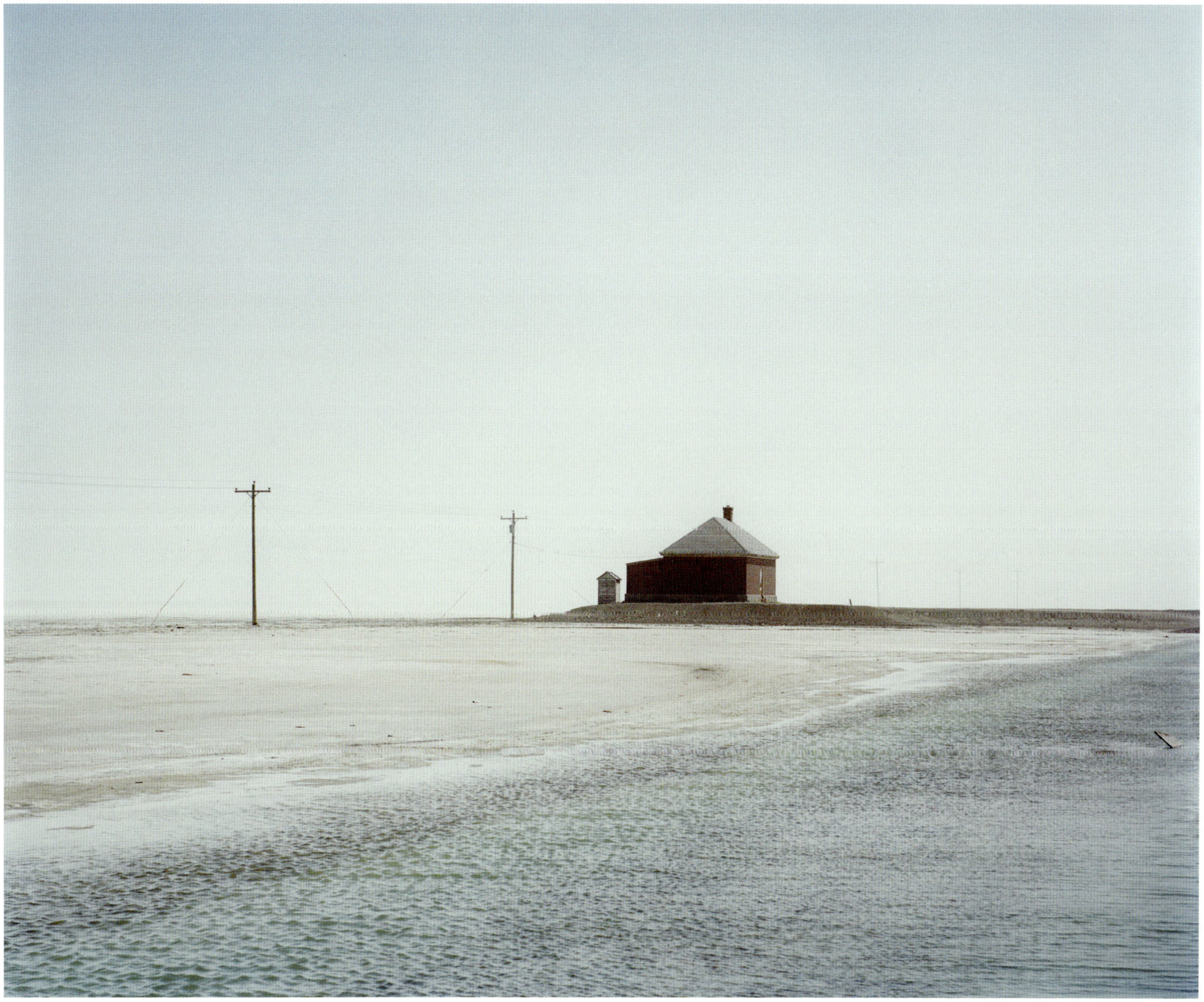

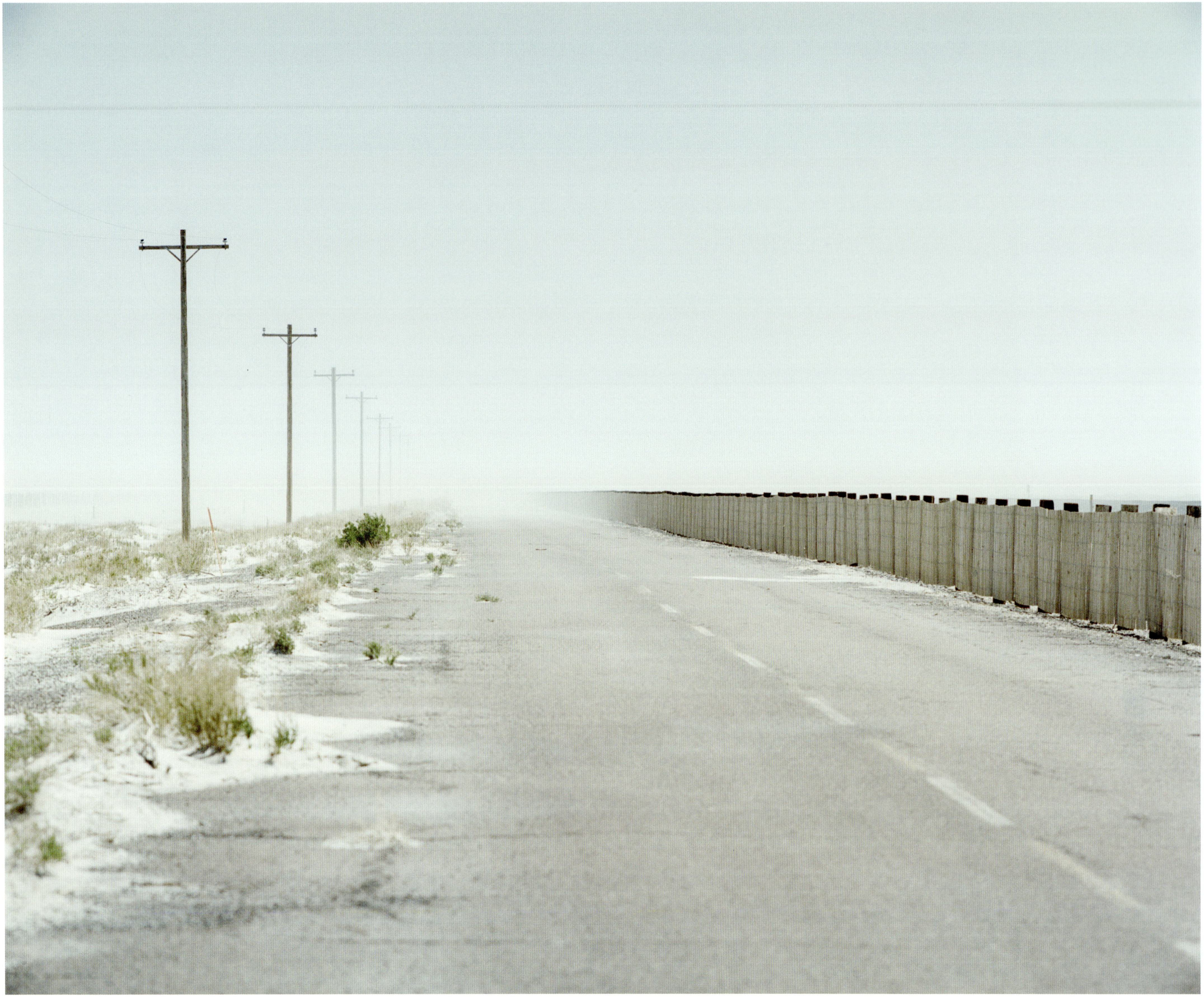

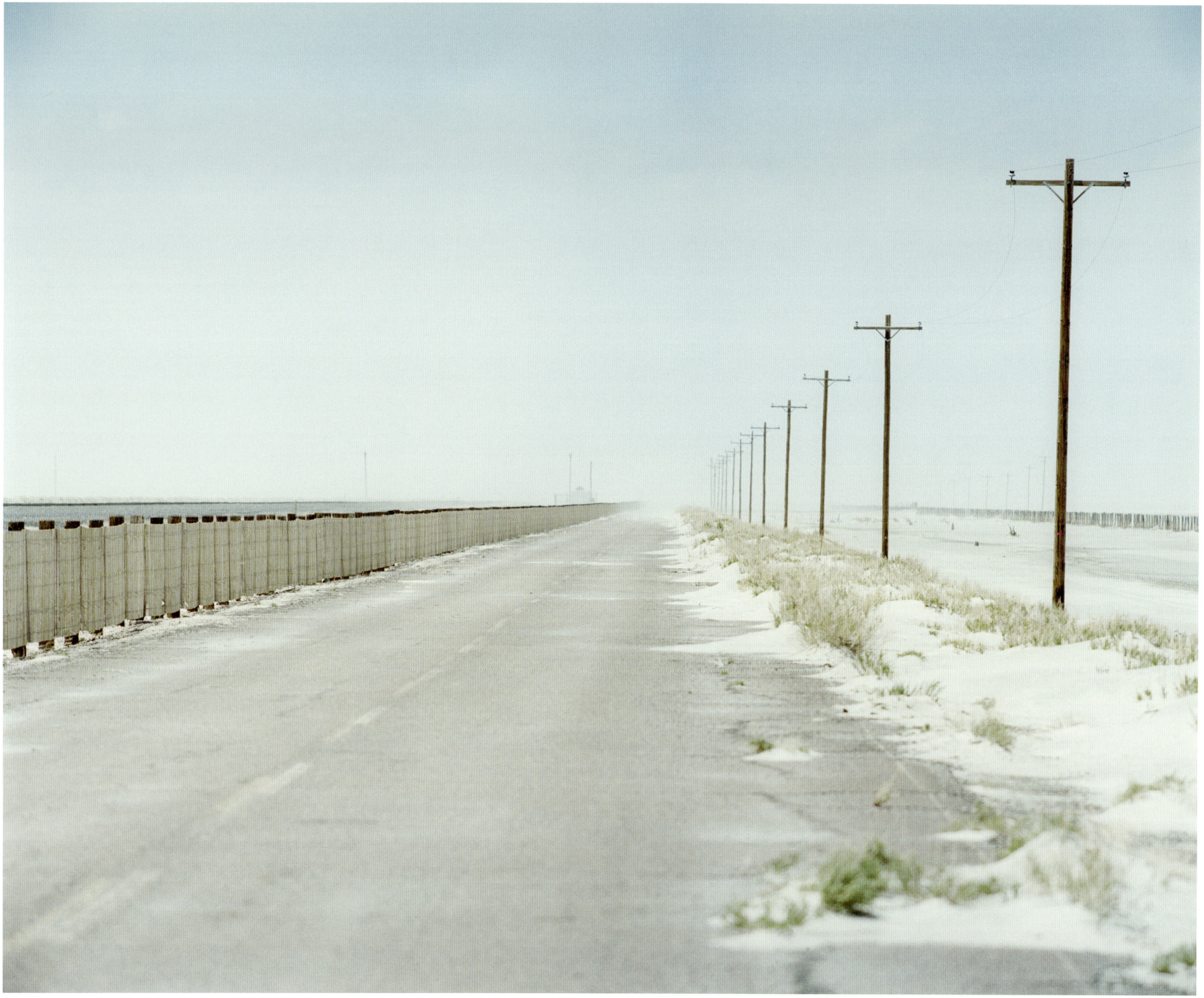

1.2, 1.3
1.4

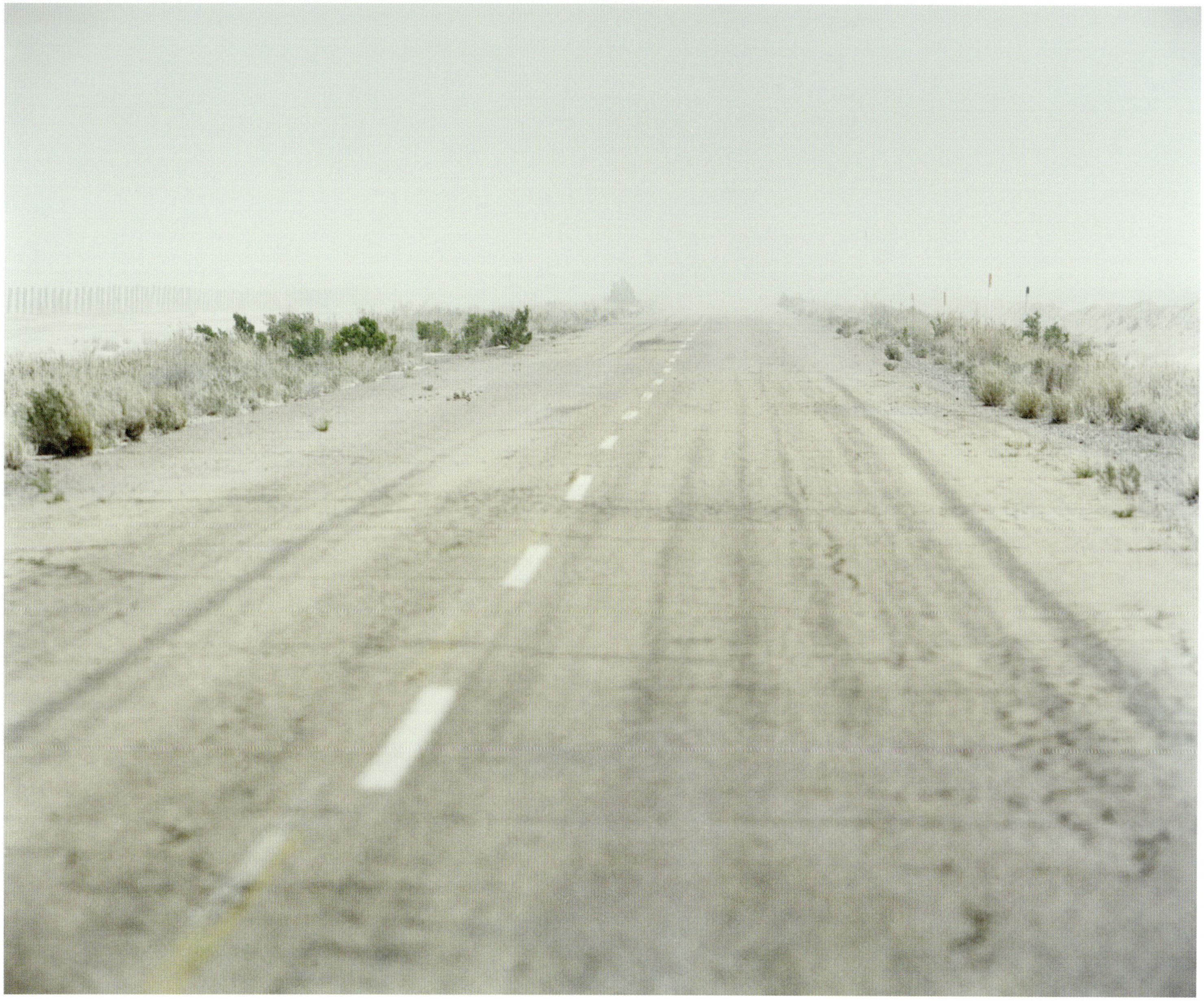

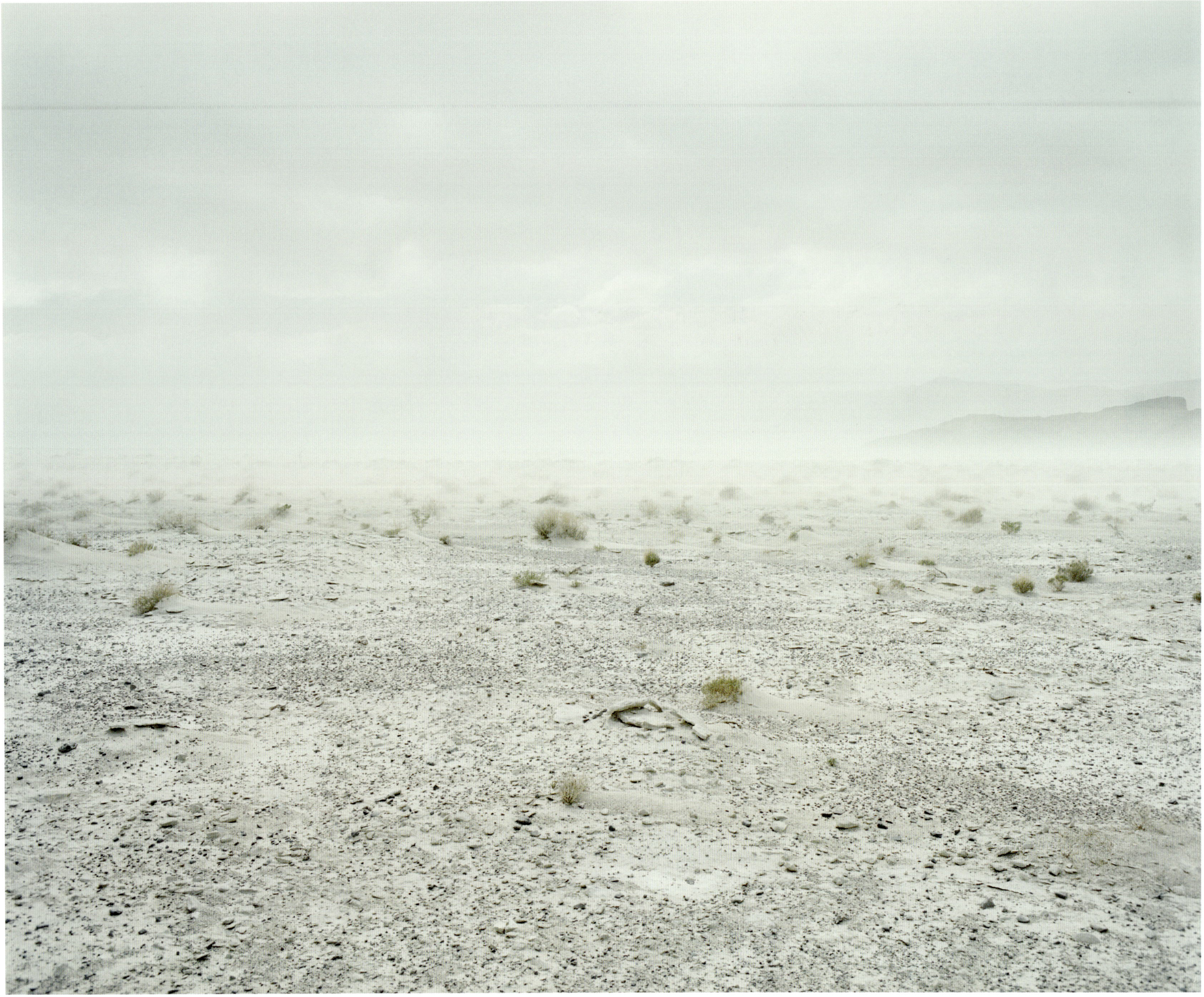

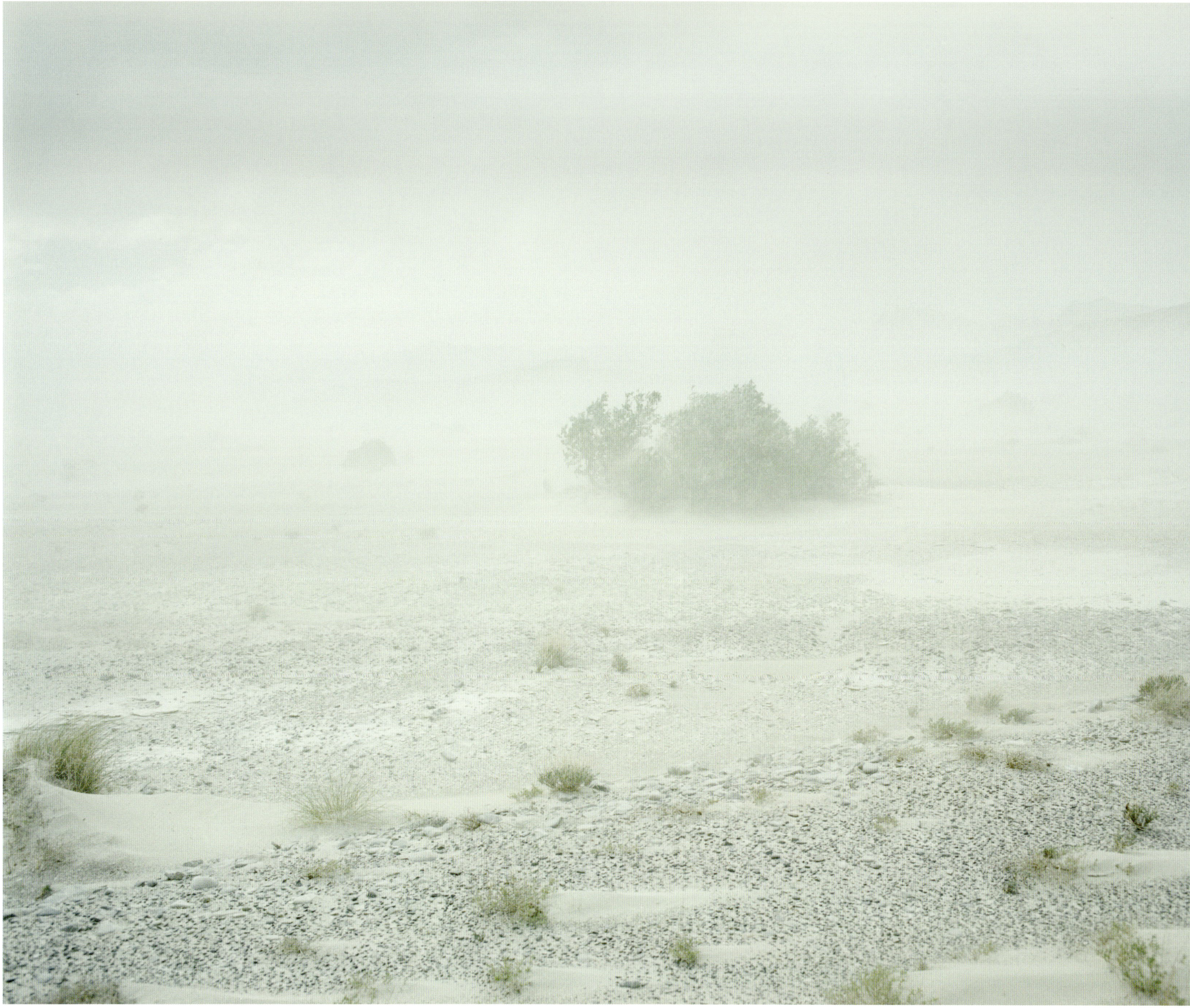

I.5, I.6
I.7

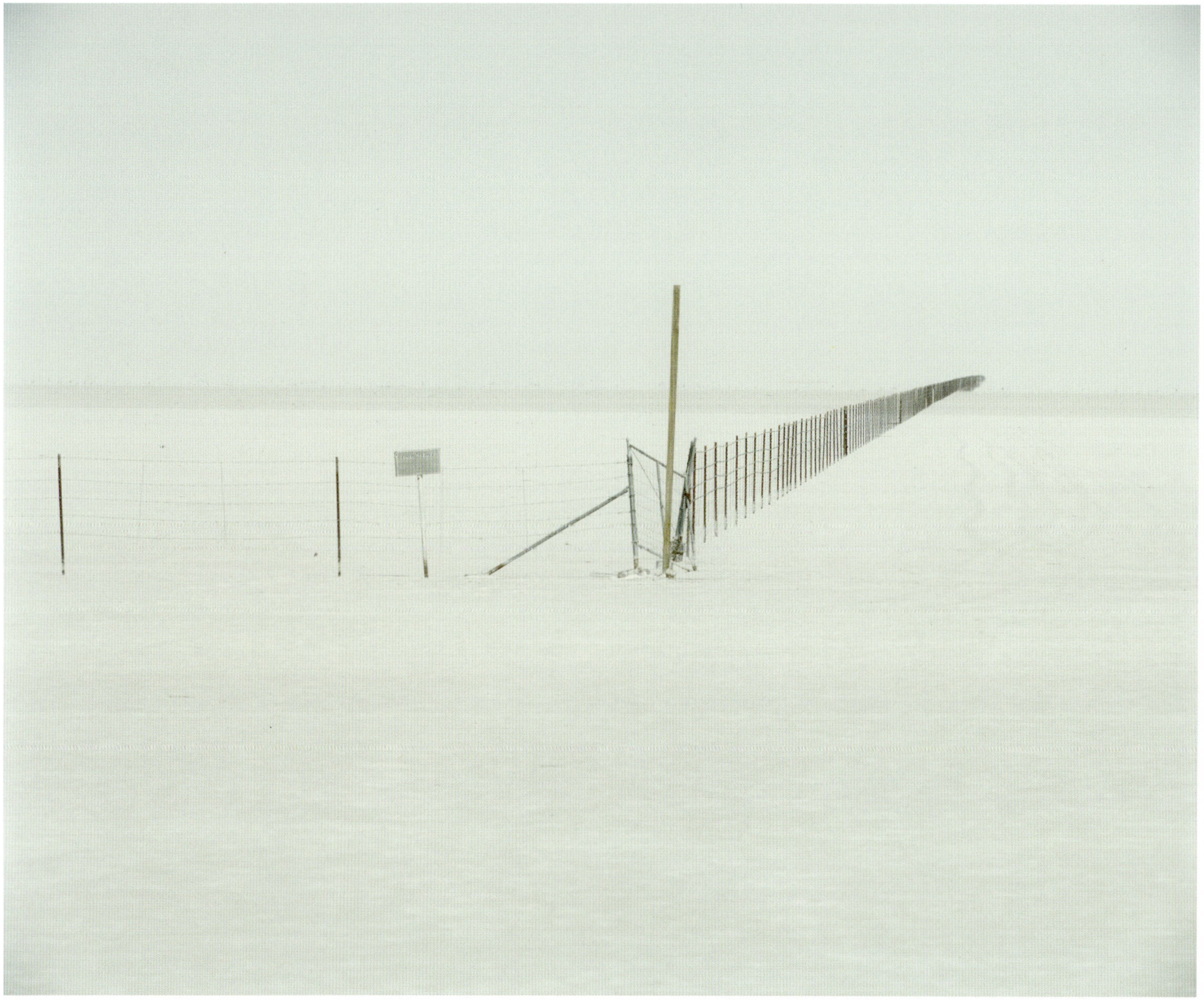

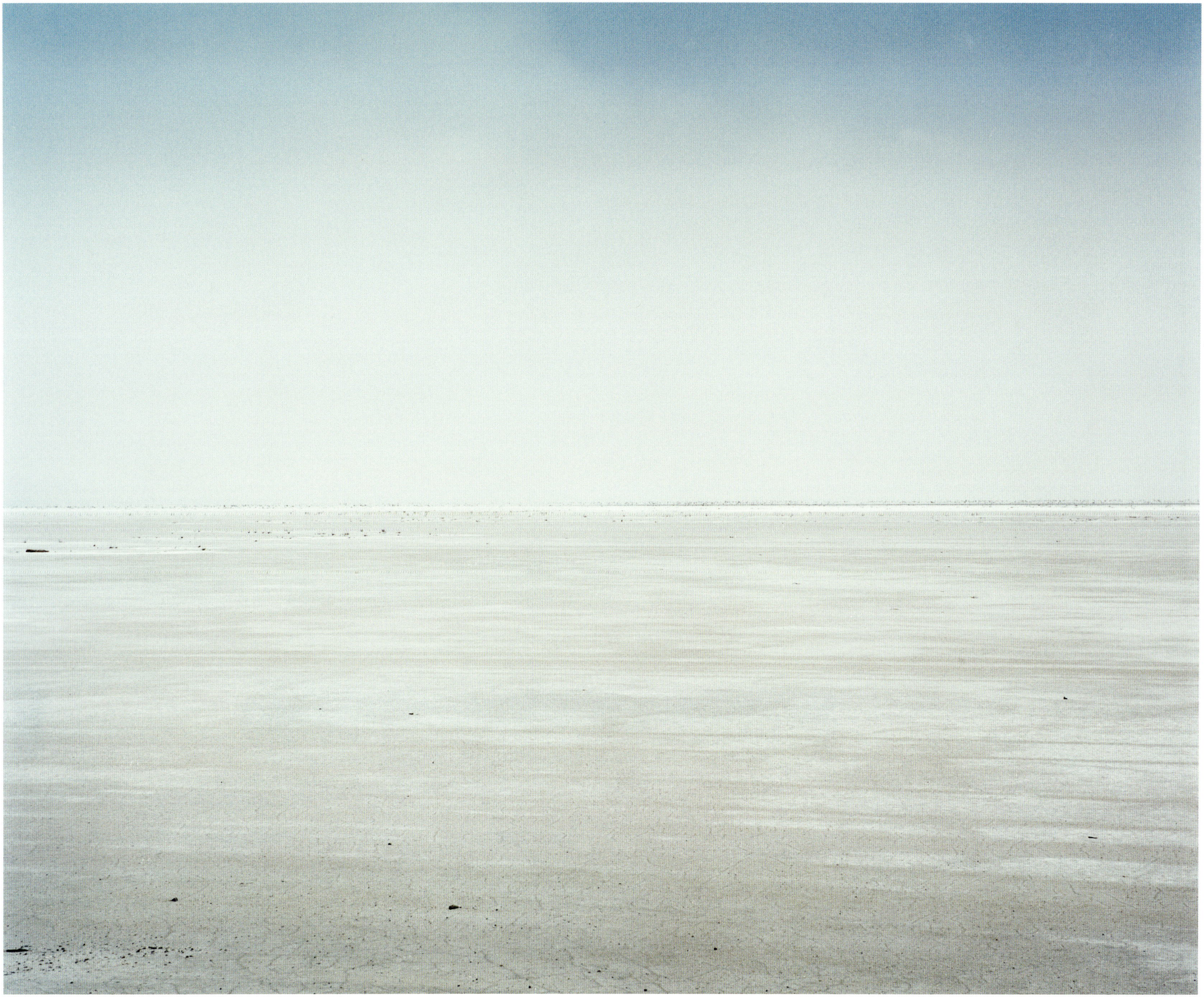

1.9

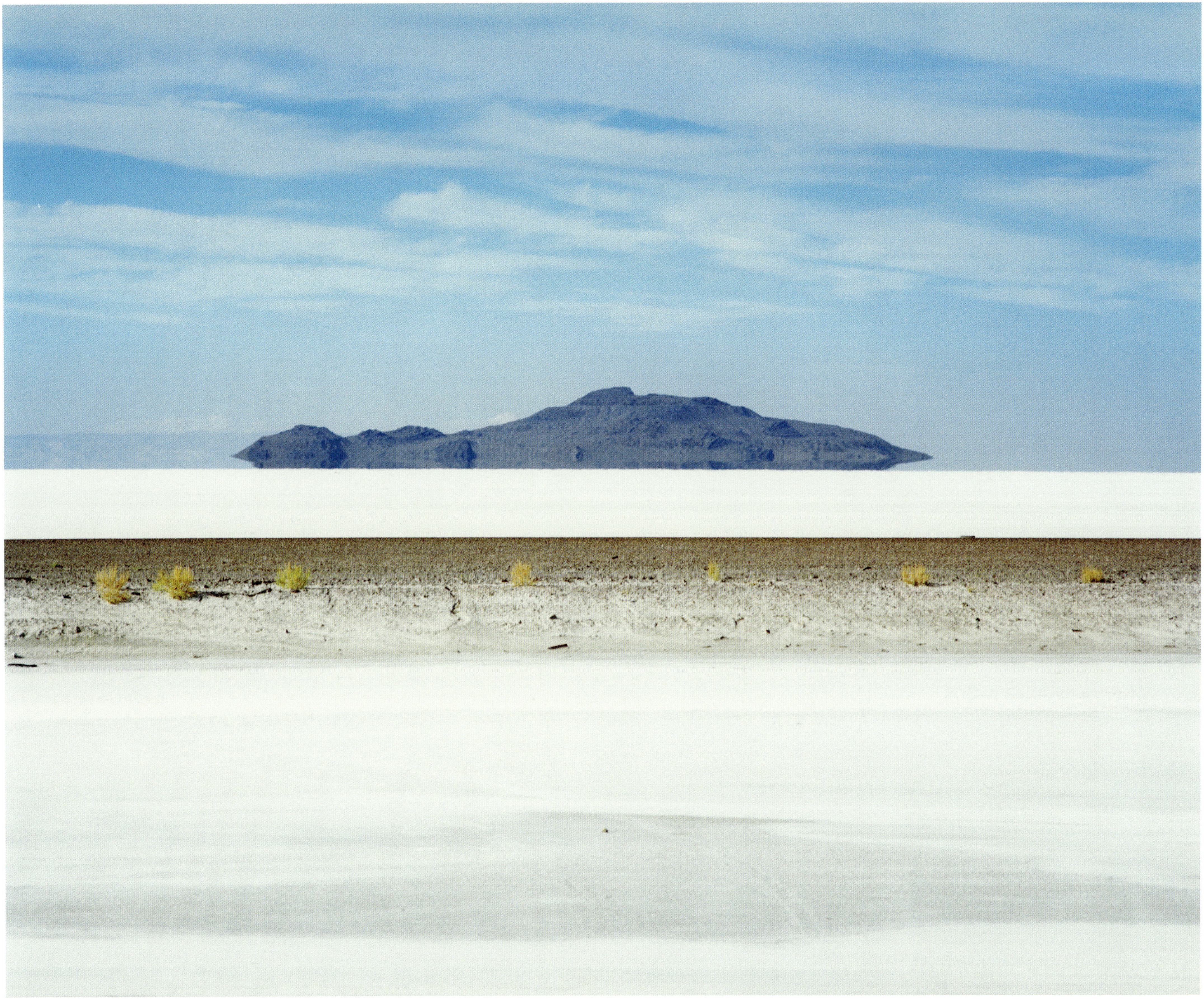

II. WENDOVER

II.1

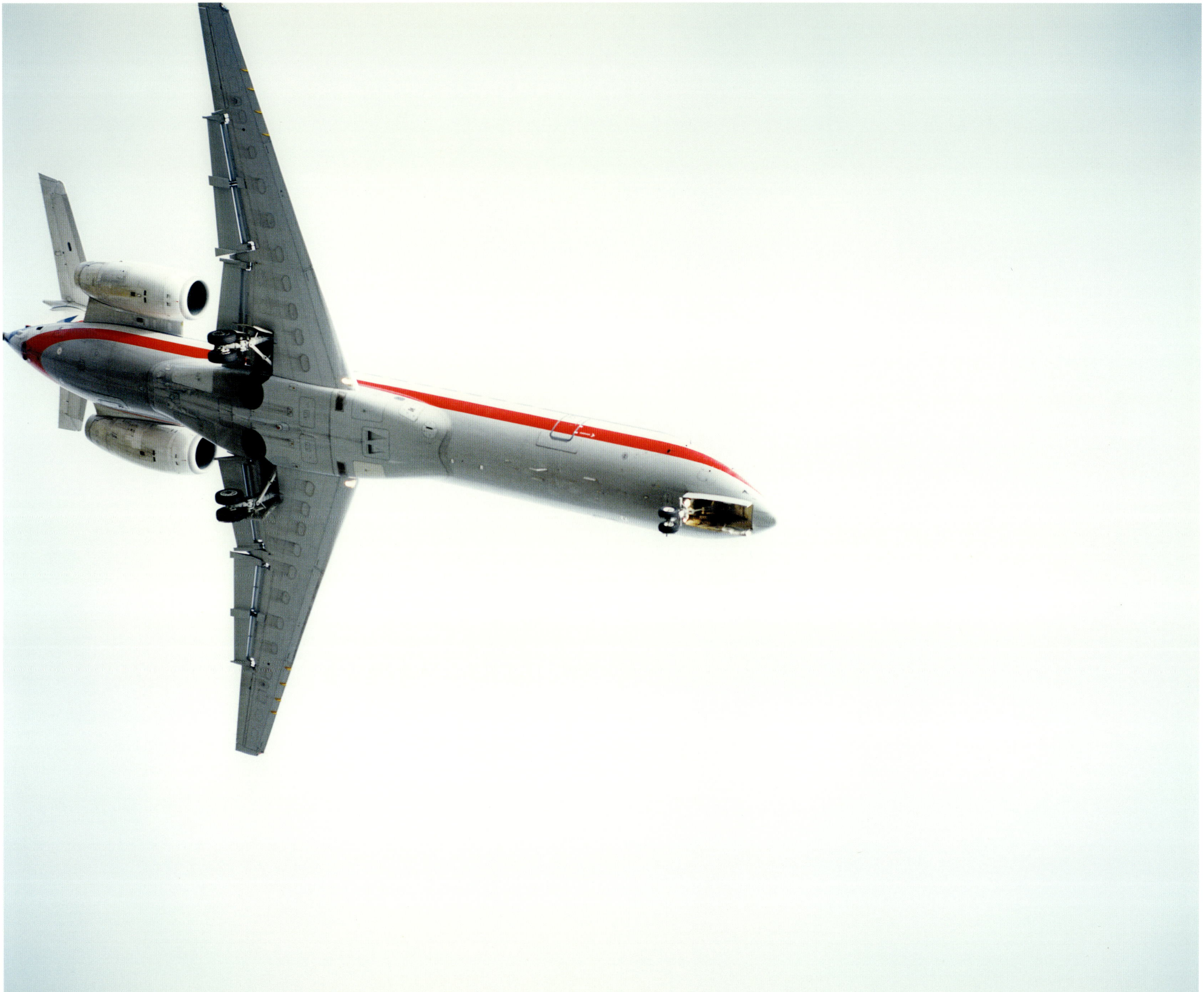

II.2

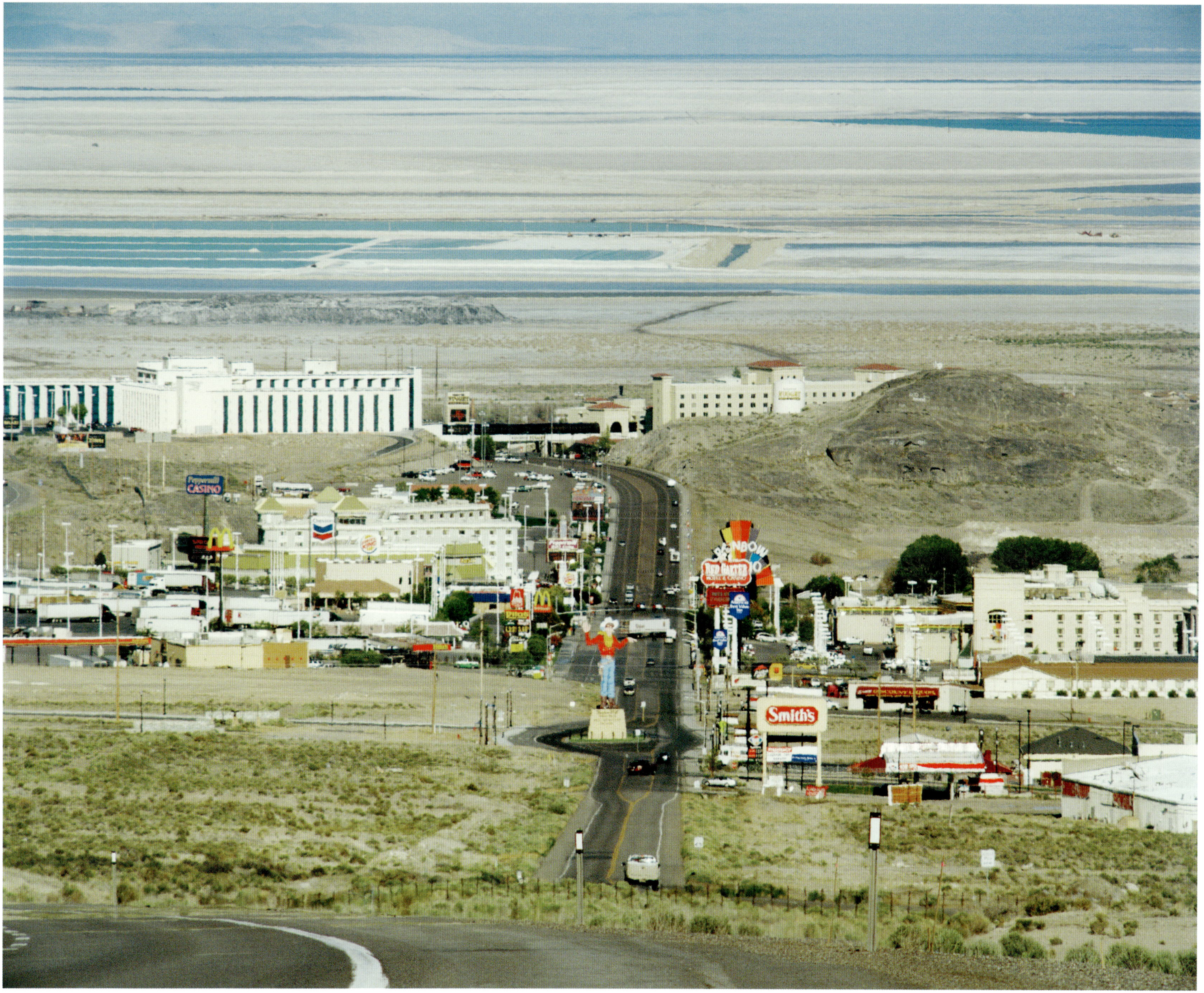
CASINO
RED GARTER
Smith's

II.3

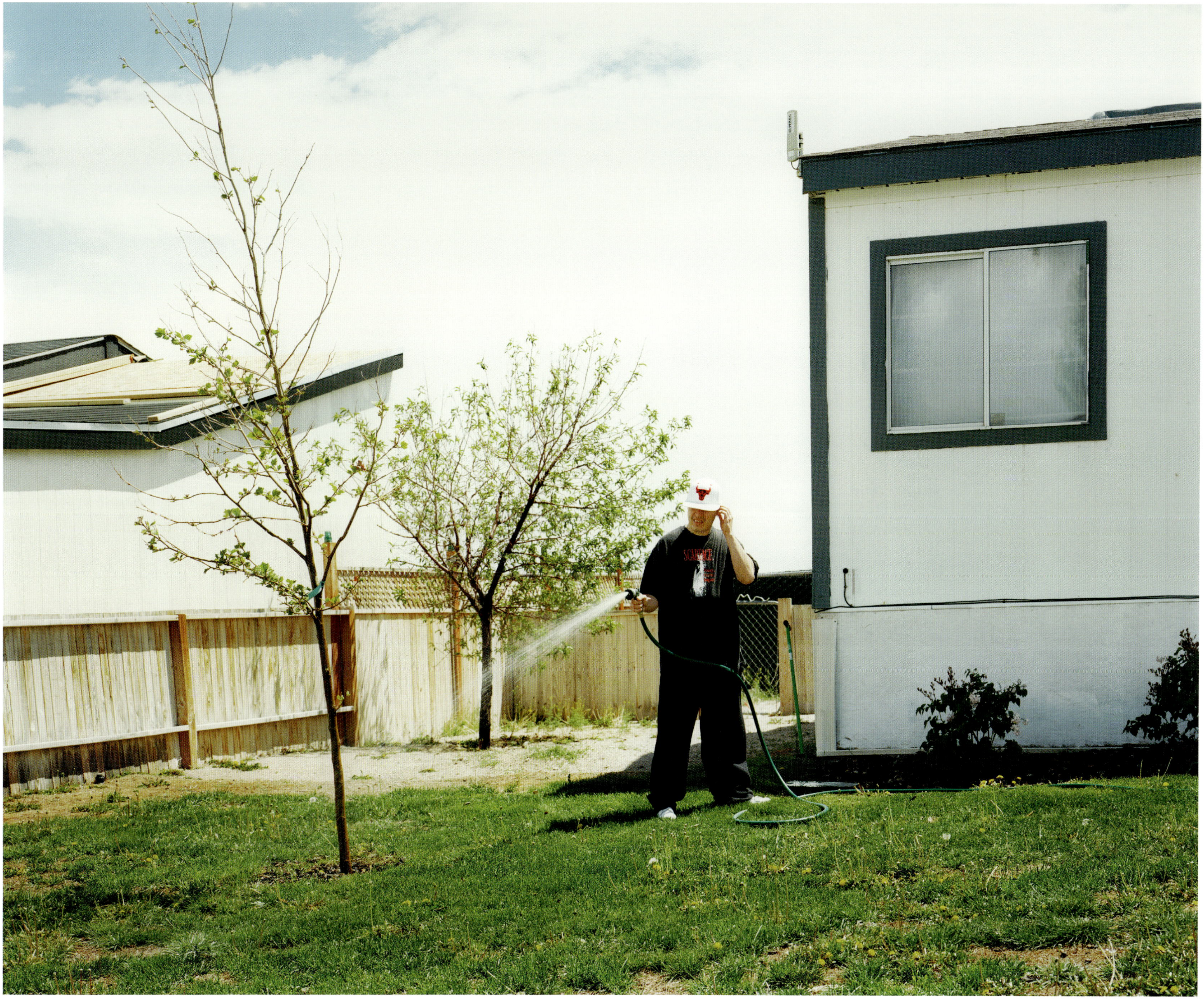

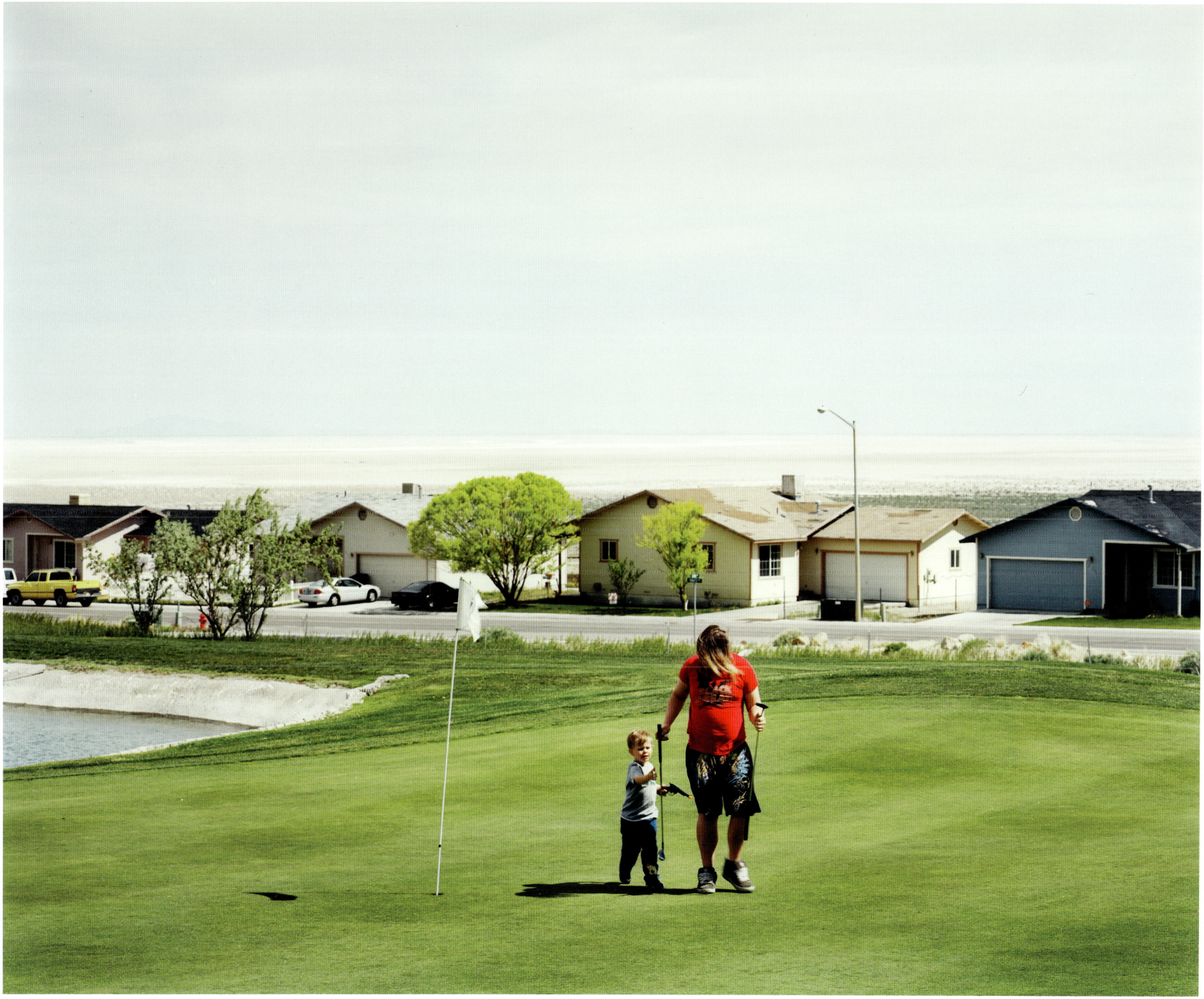

II.5

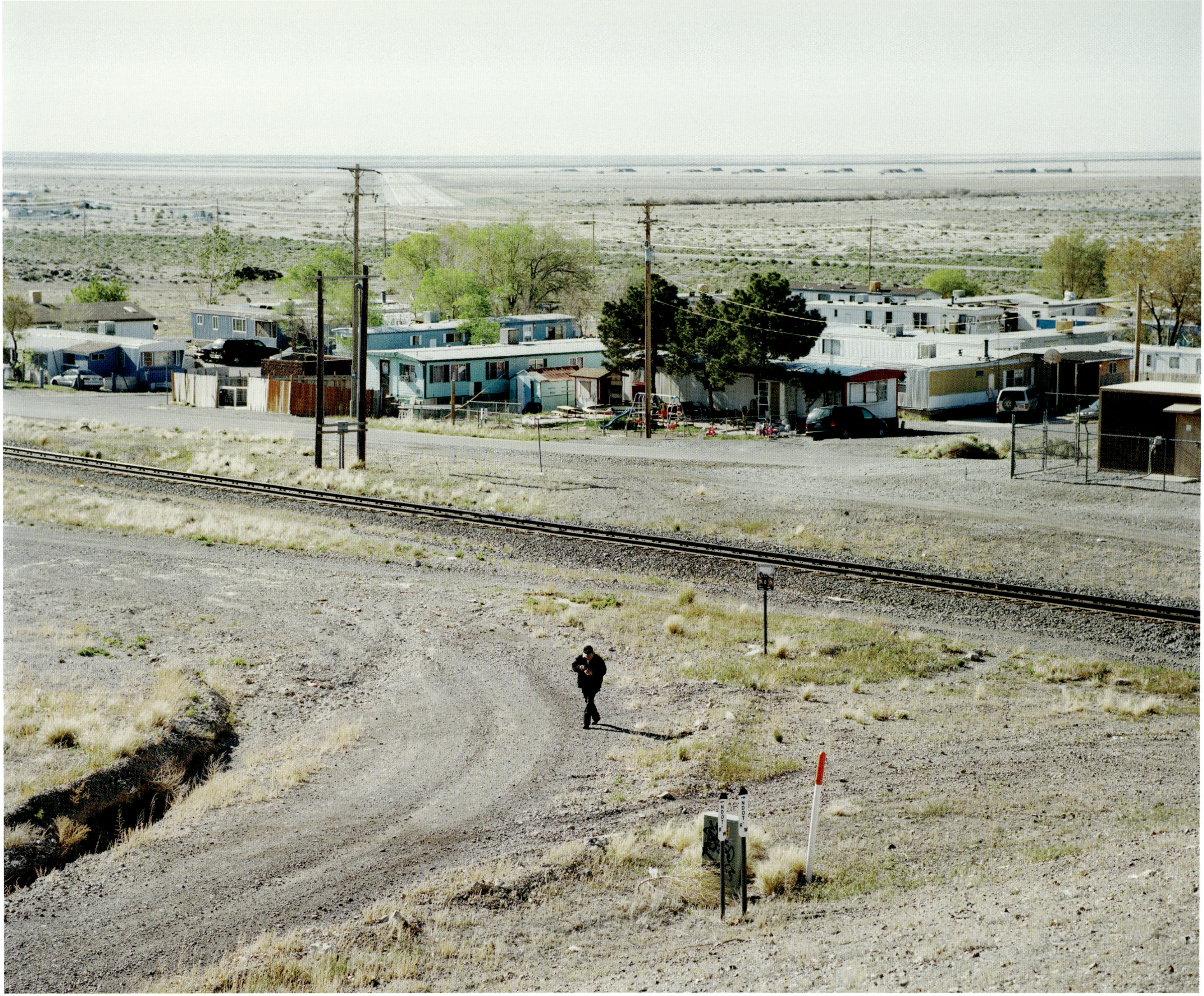

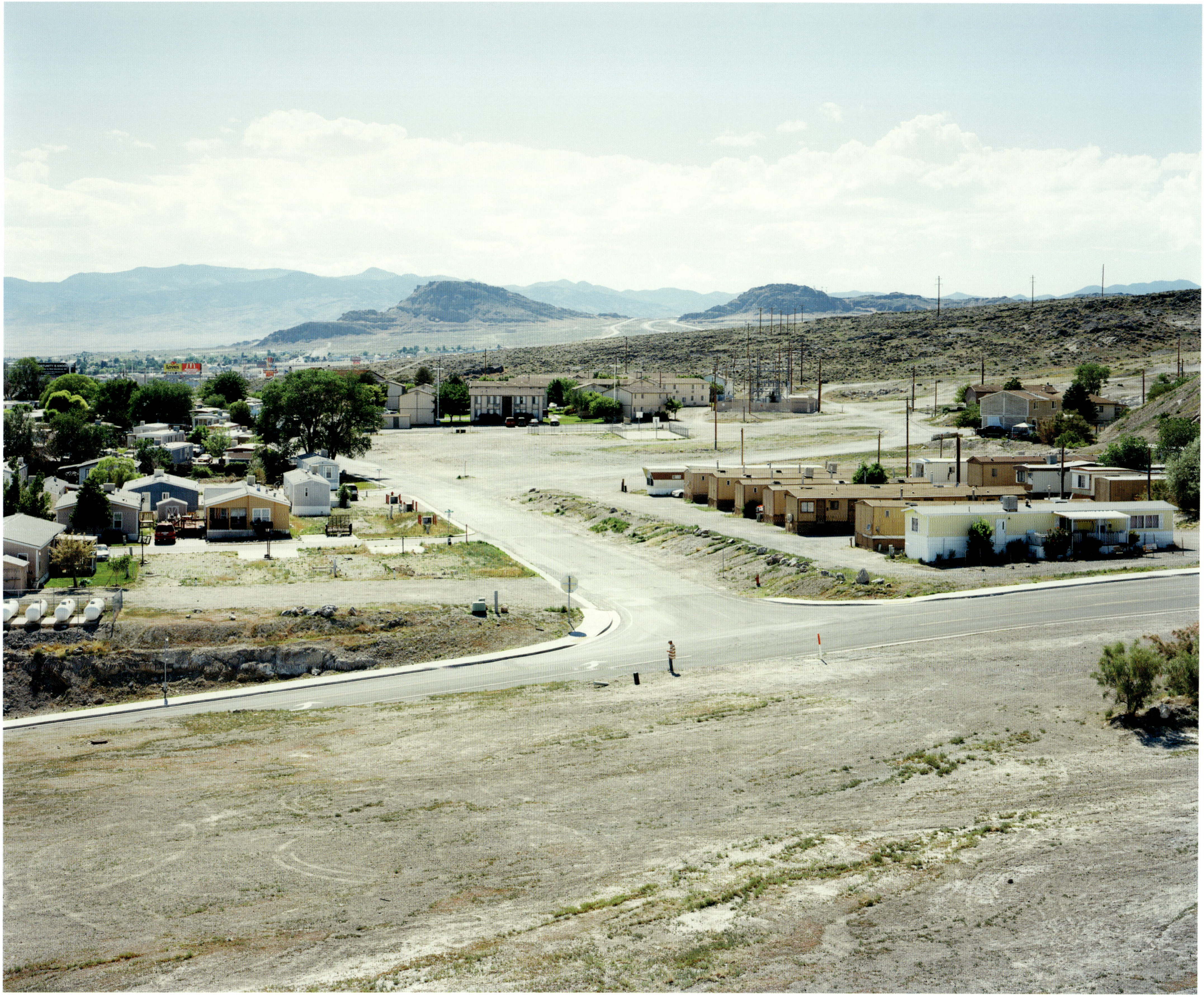

II.7

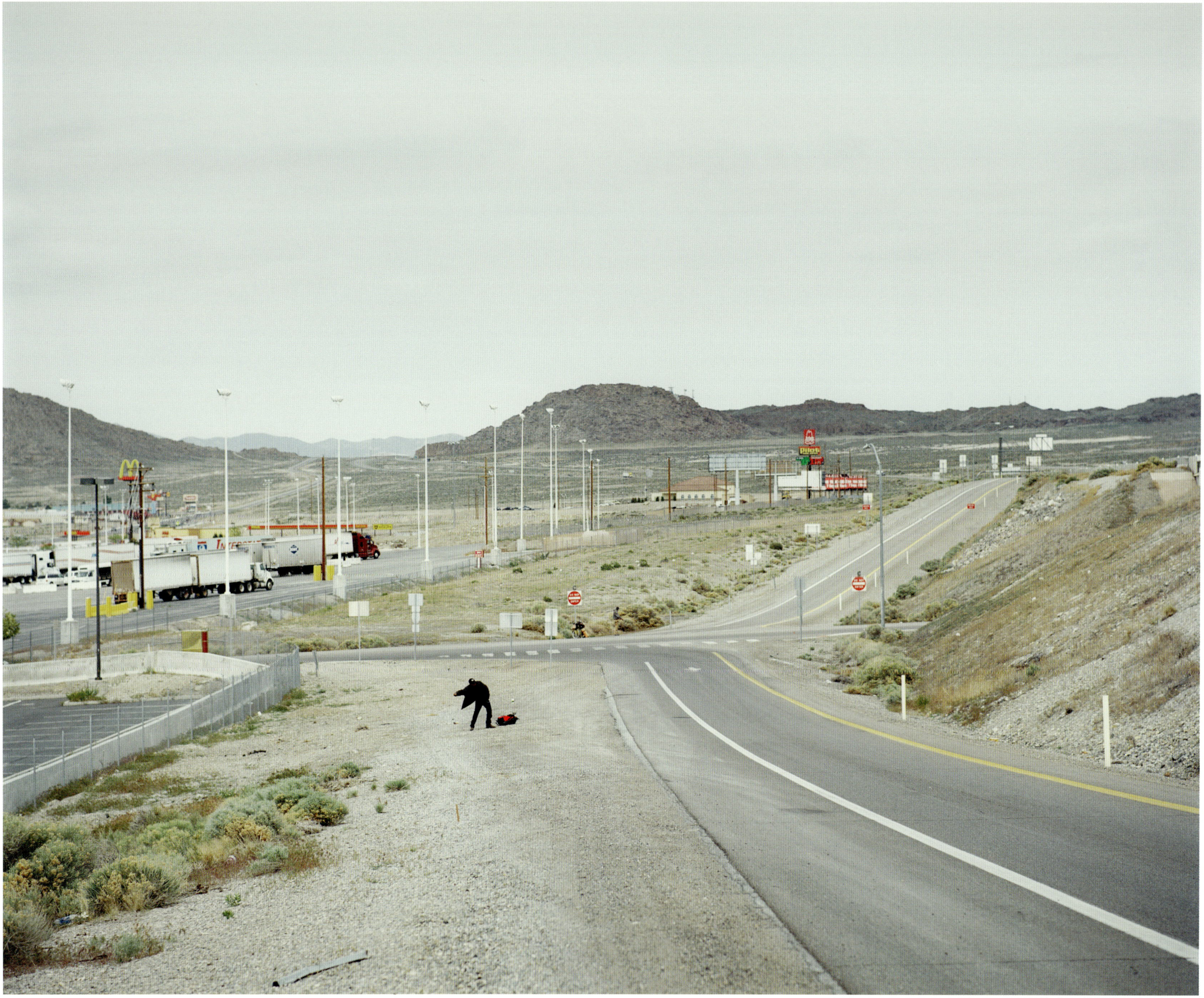

III. MONTEGO BAY

III.1

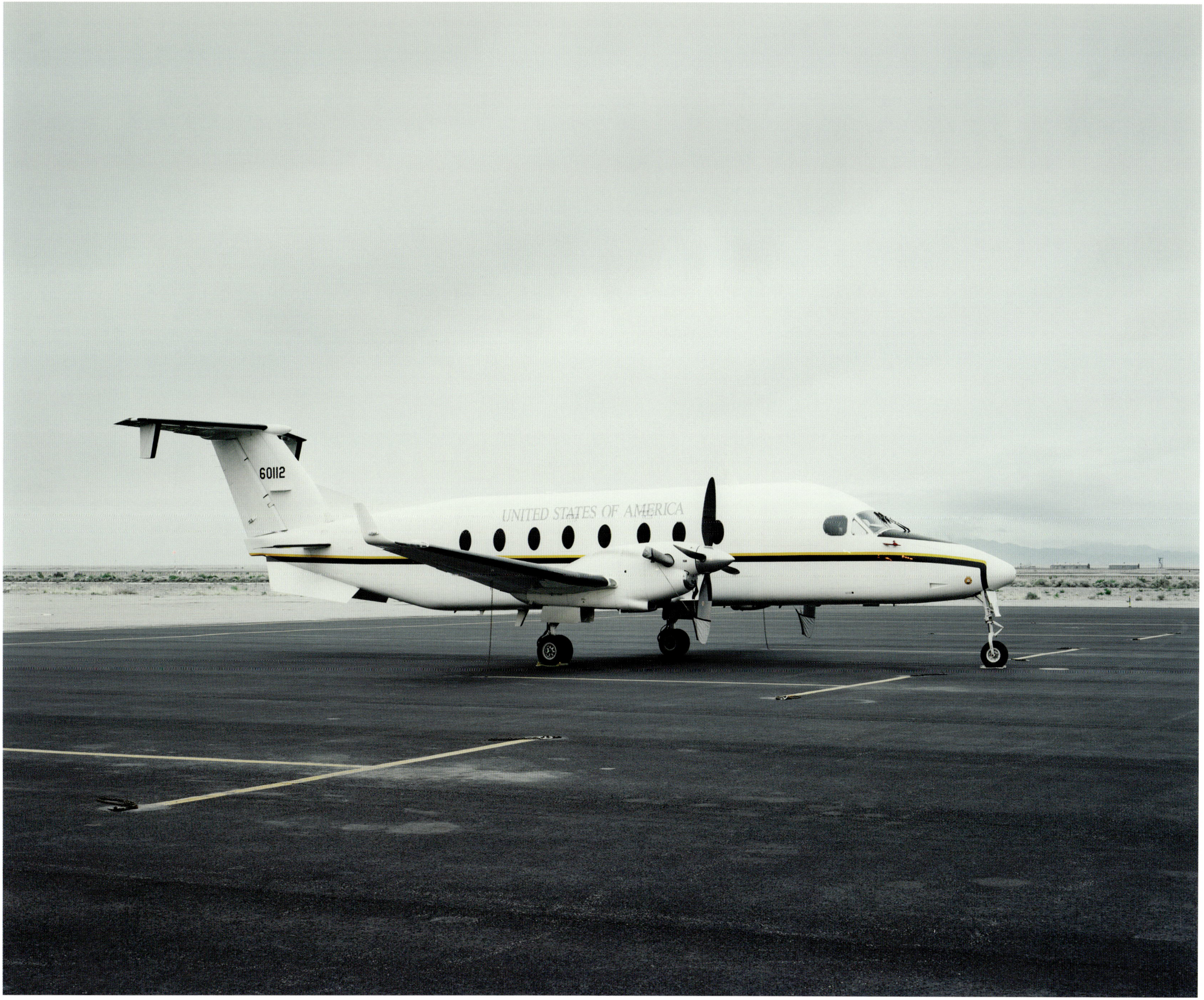
60112
UNITED STATES OF AMERICA

III.2

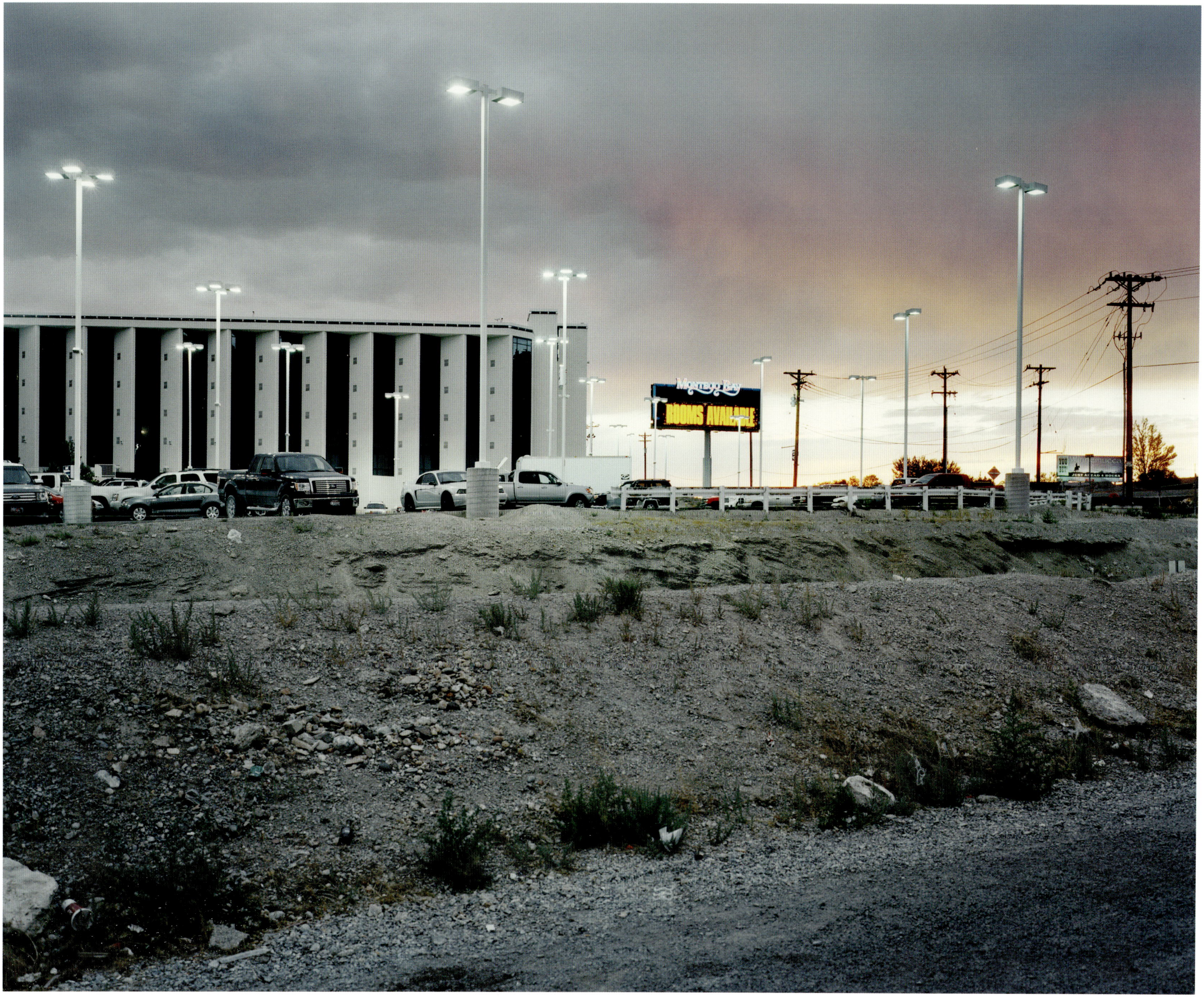
Montego Bay
ROOMS AVAILABLE

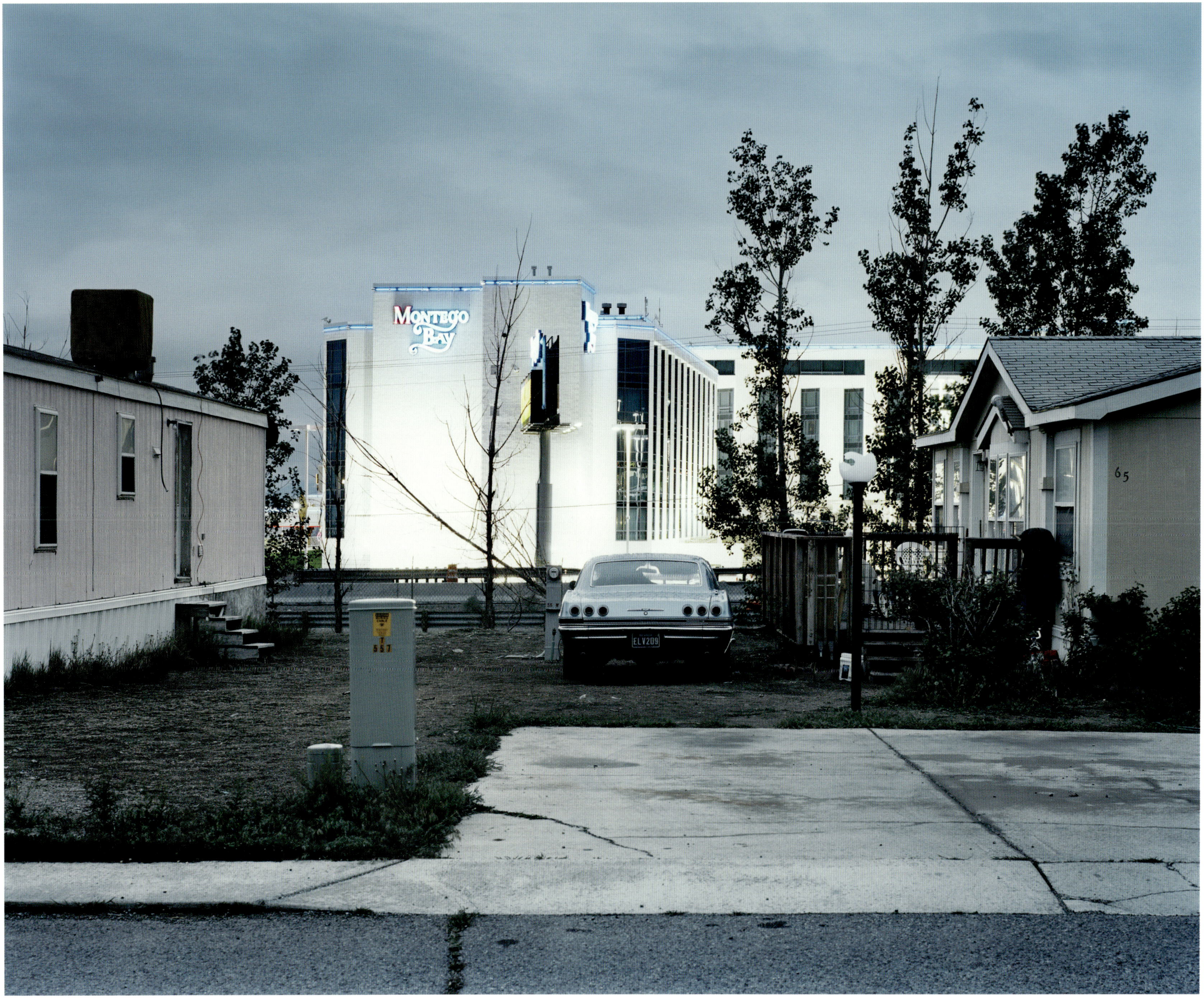
MONTEGO
BAY
65
ELV209
557

III.4

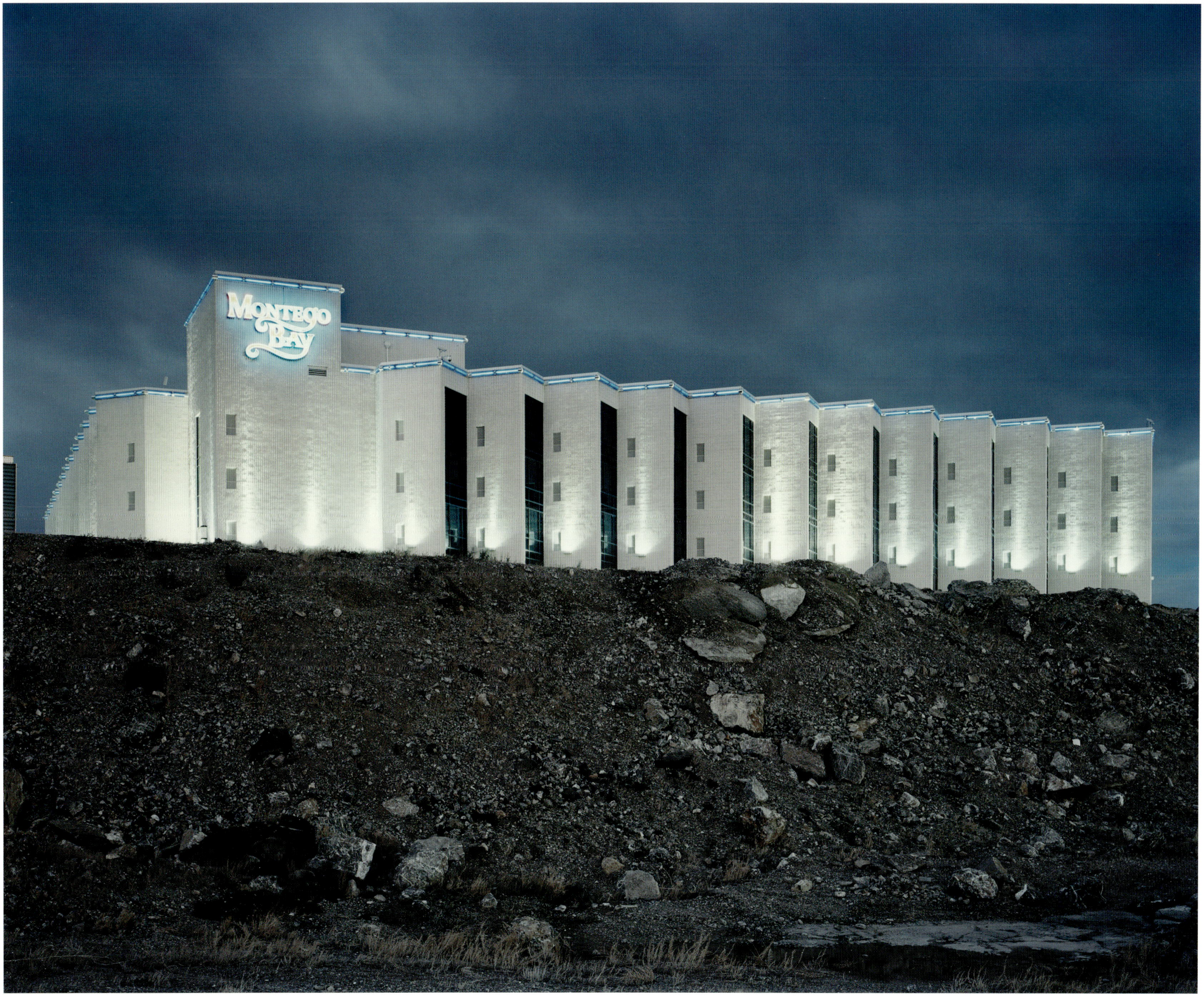
Montego
Bay

III.5

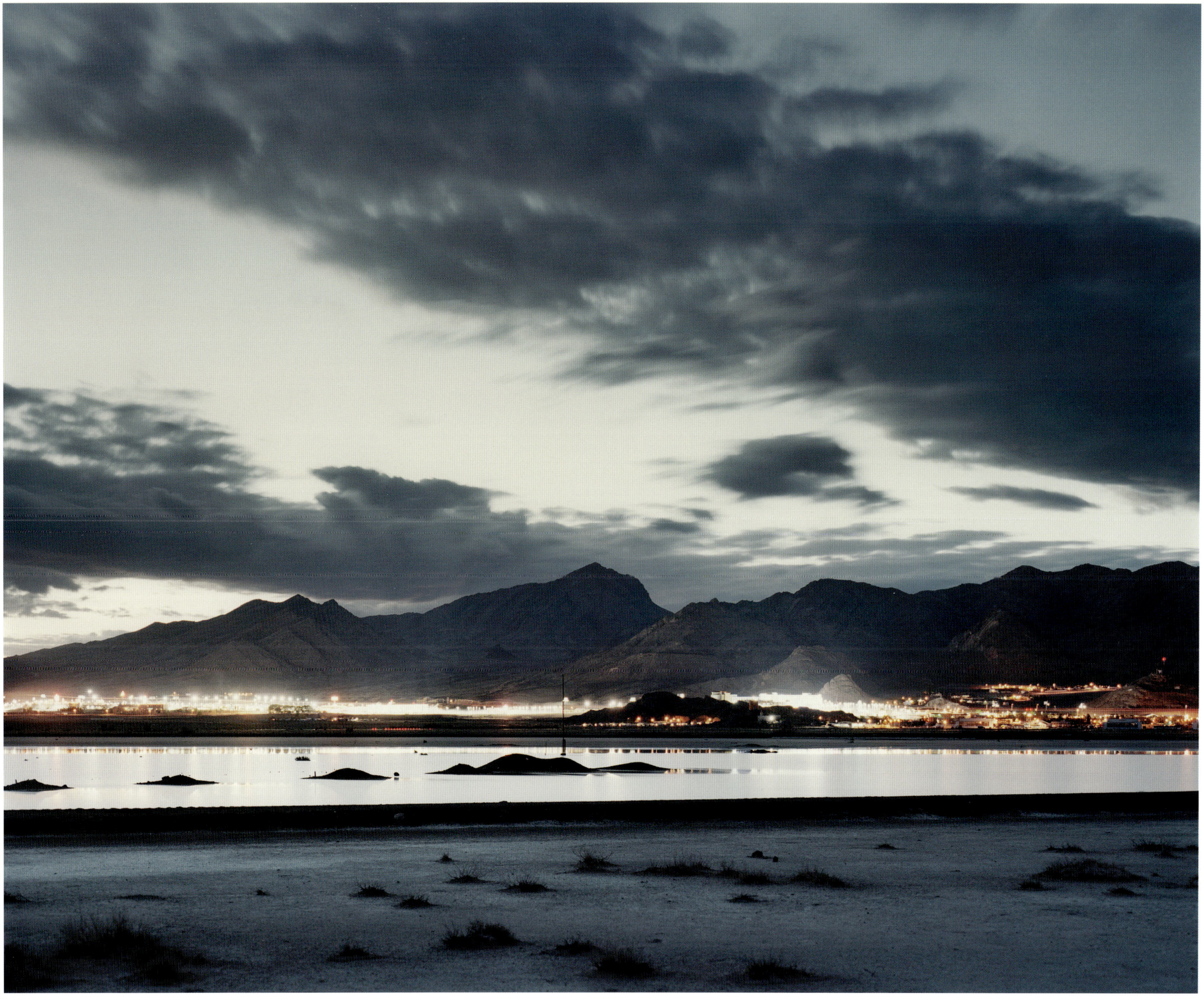

IV. SOUTHBASE

IV.1

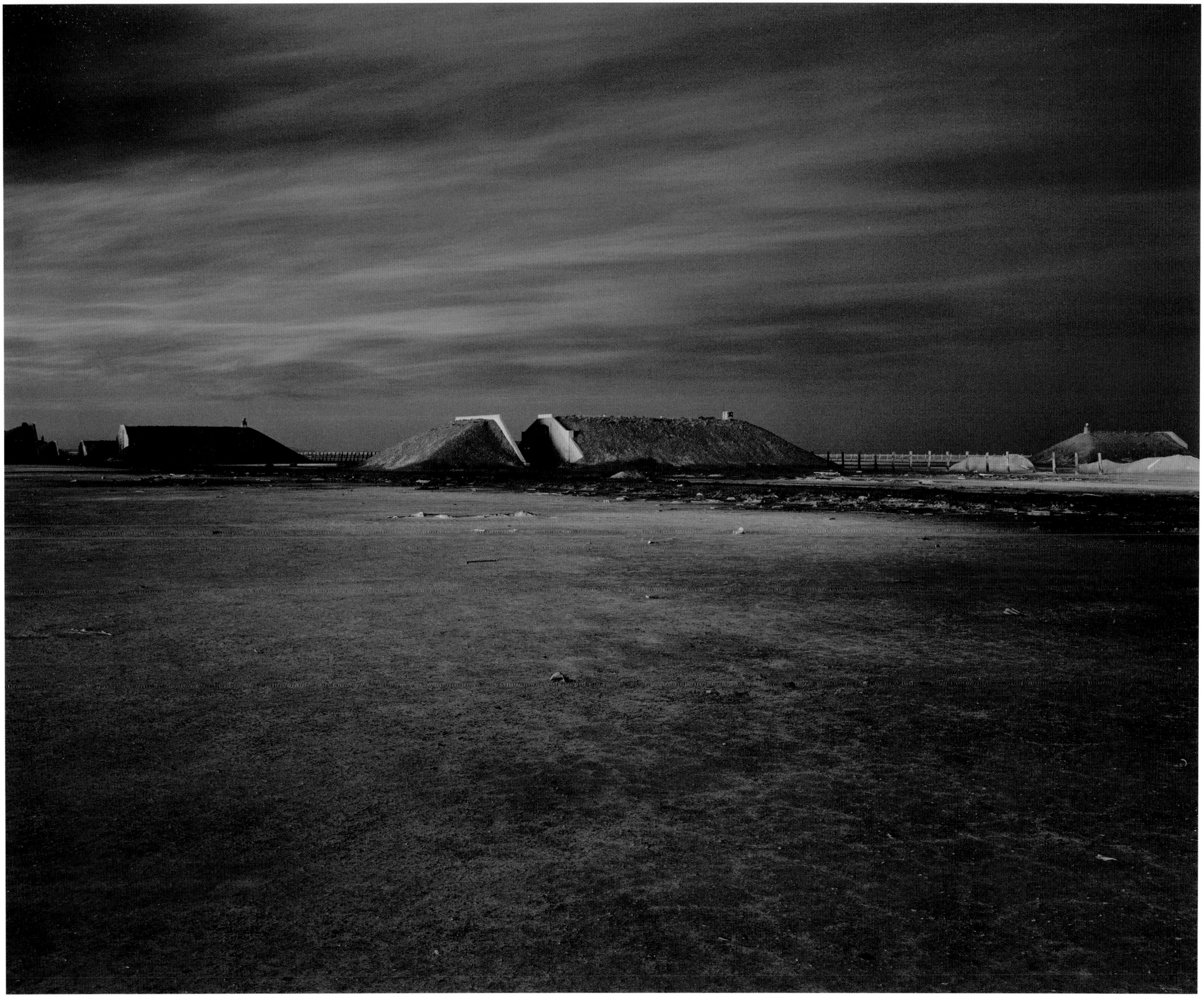

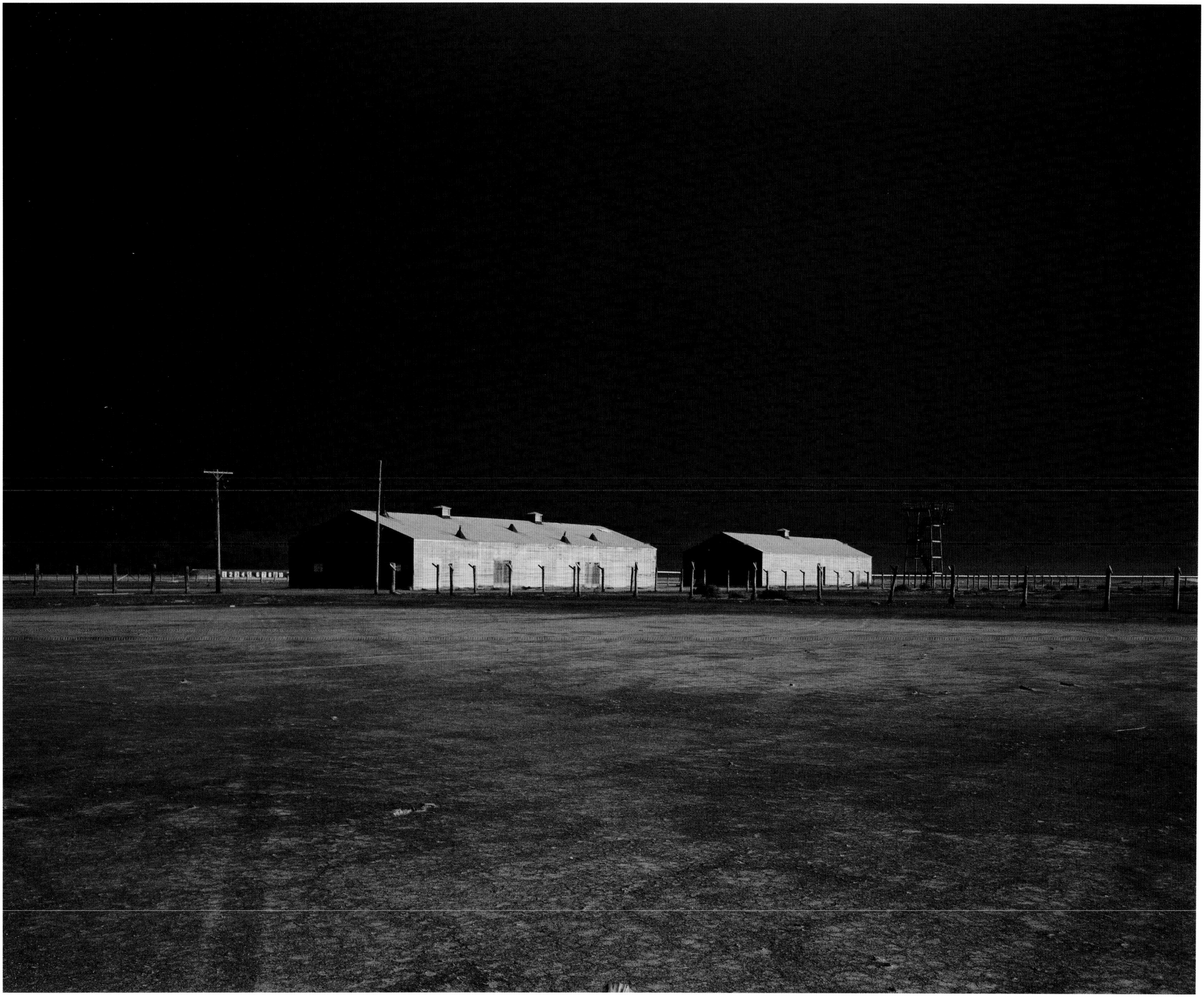

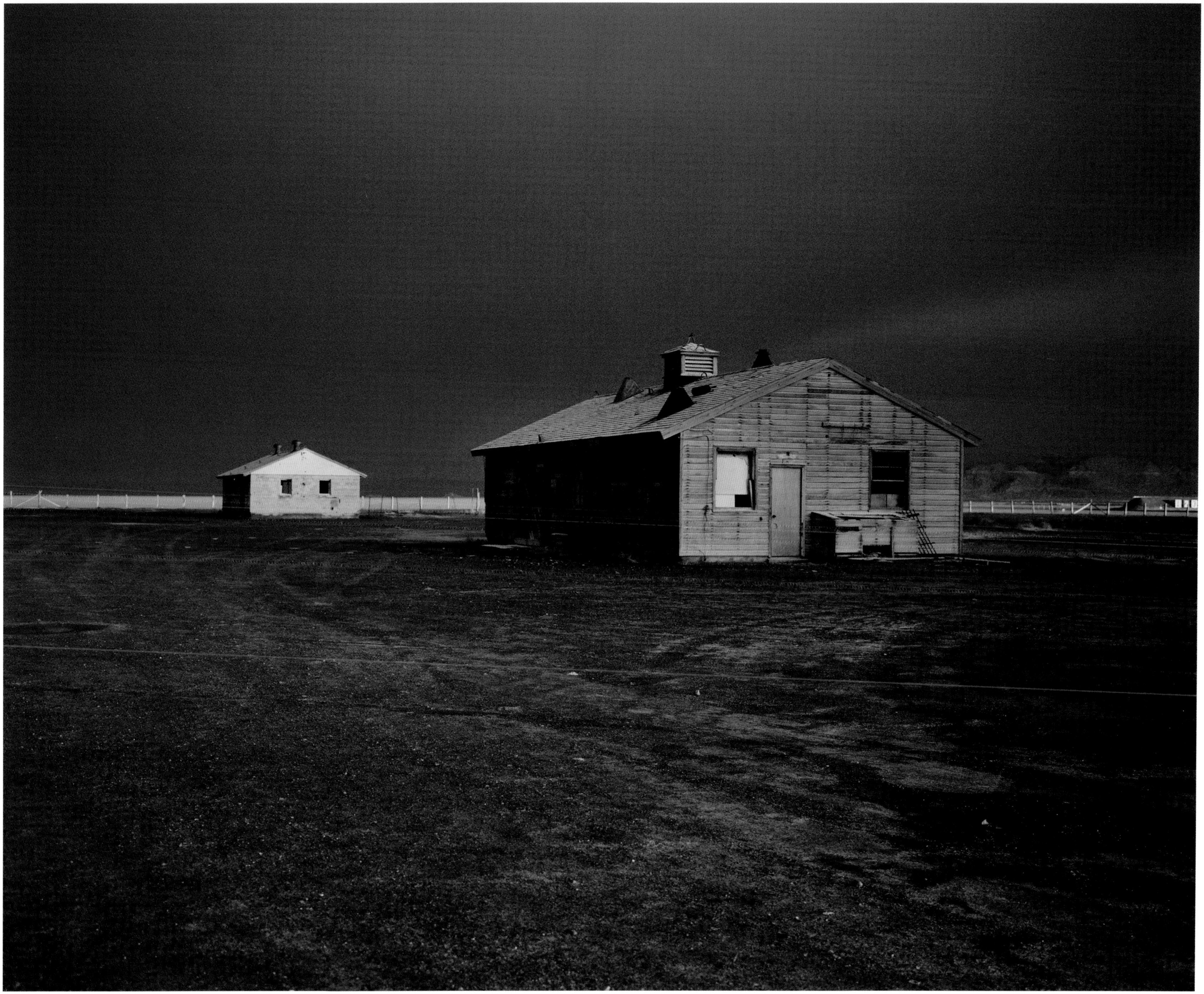

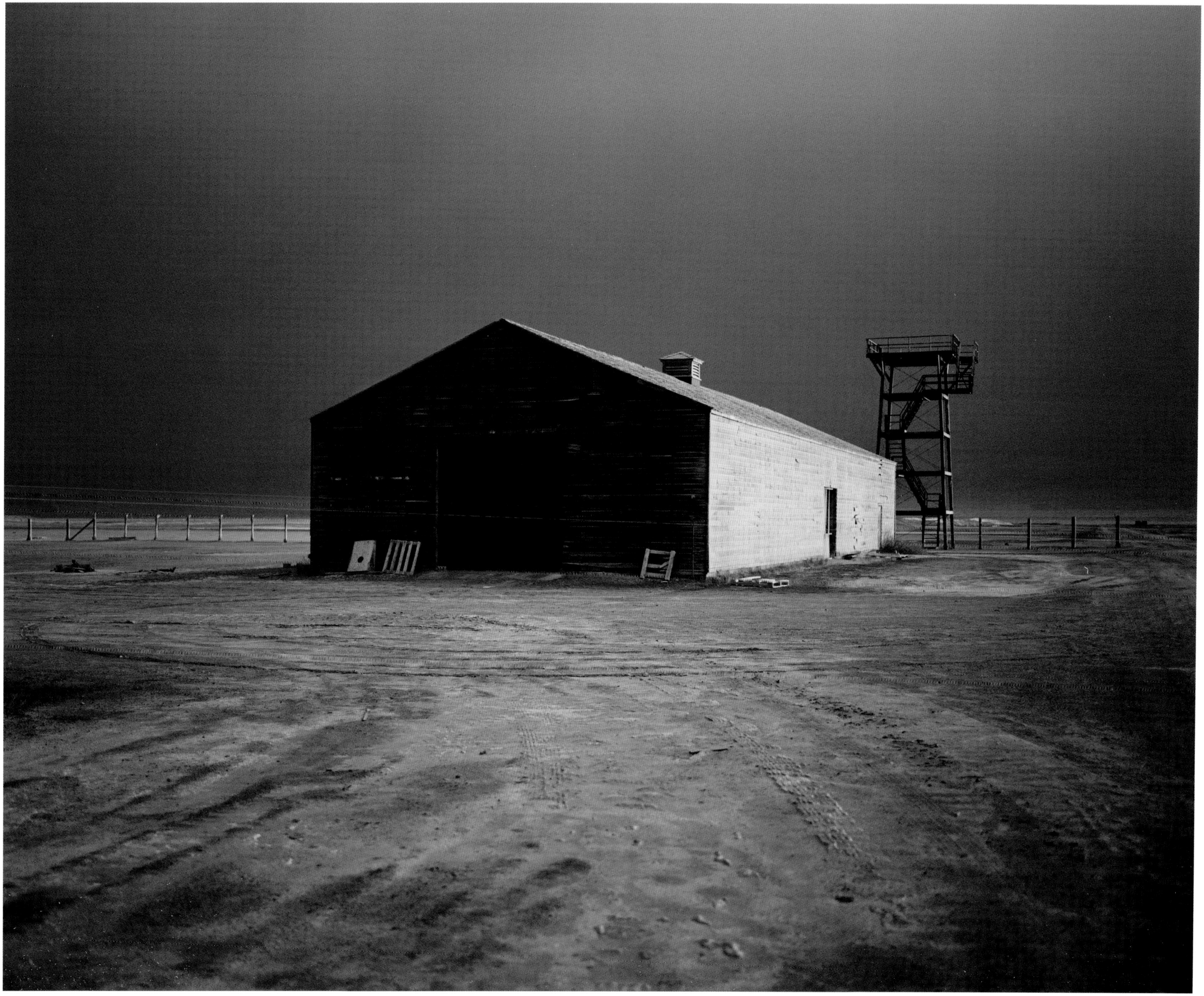

IV.5

V. UTTR

V.1

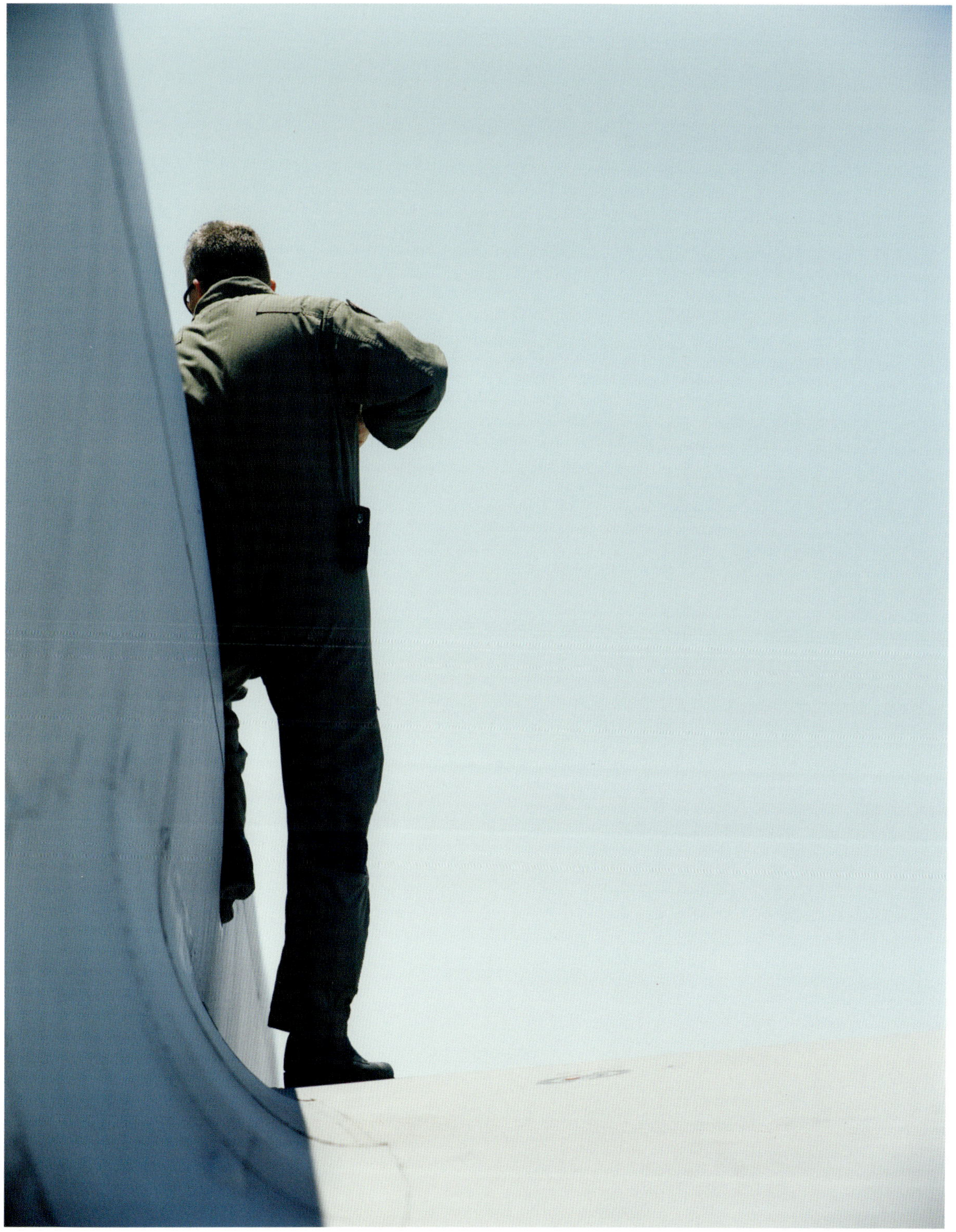

V.2

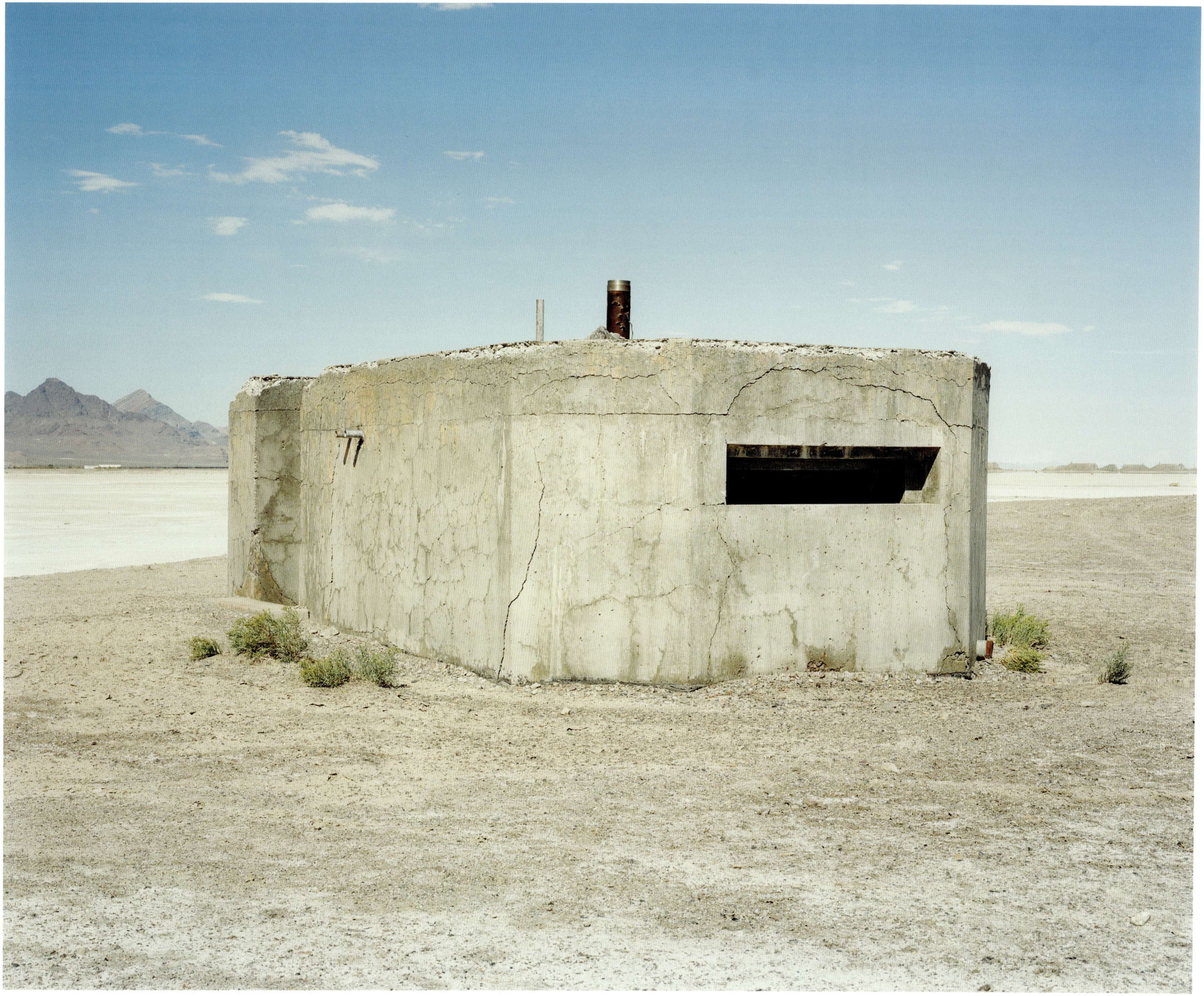

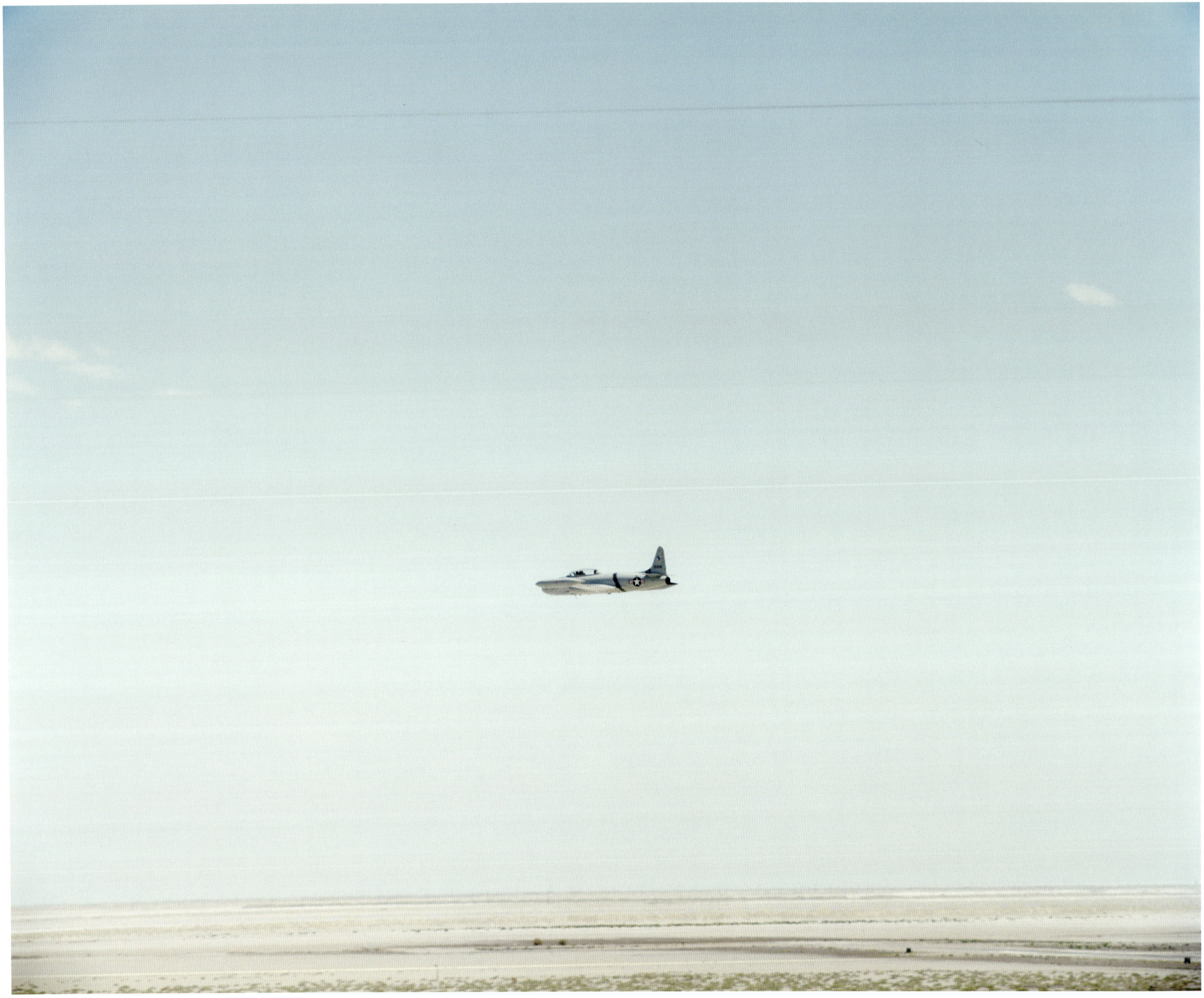

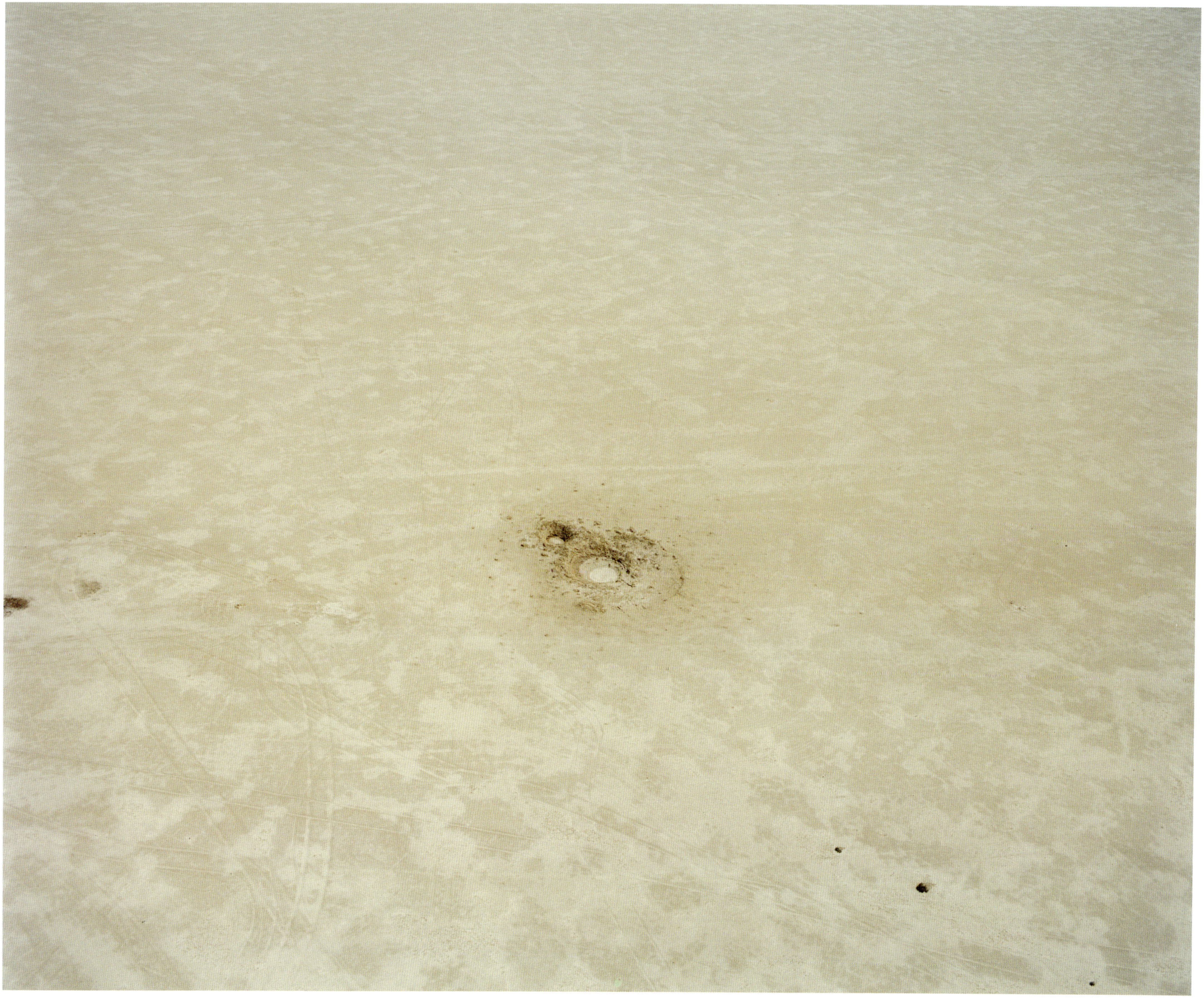

V.3, V.4
V.5

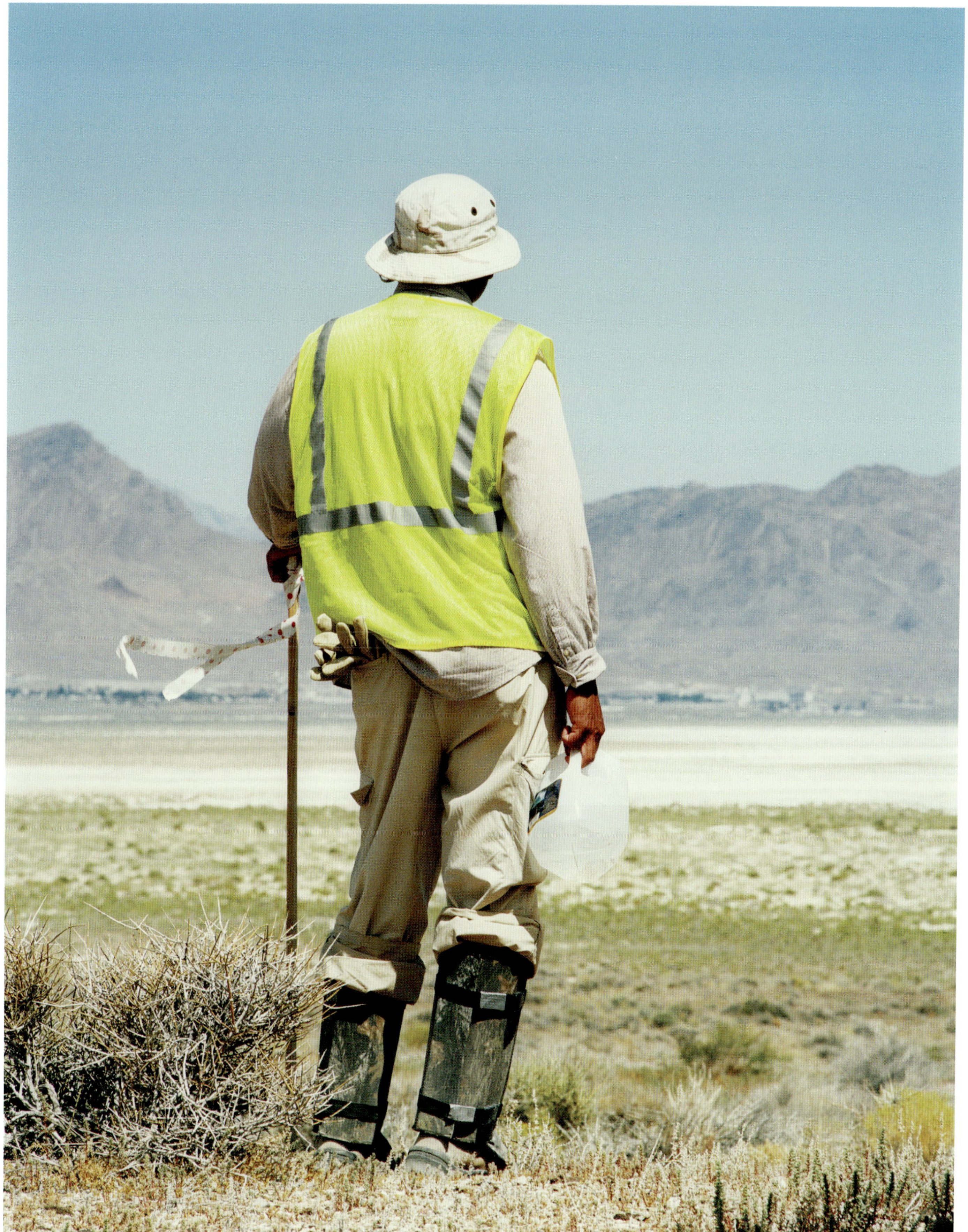

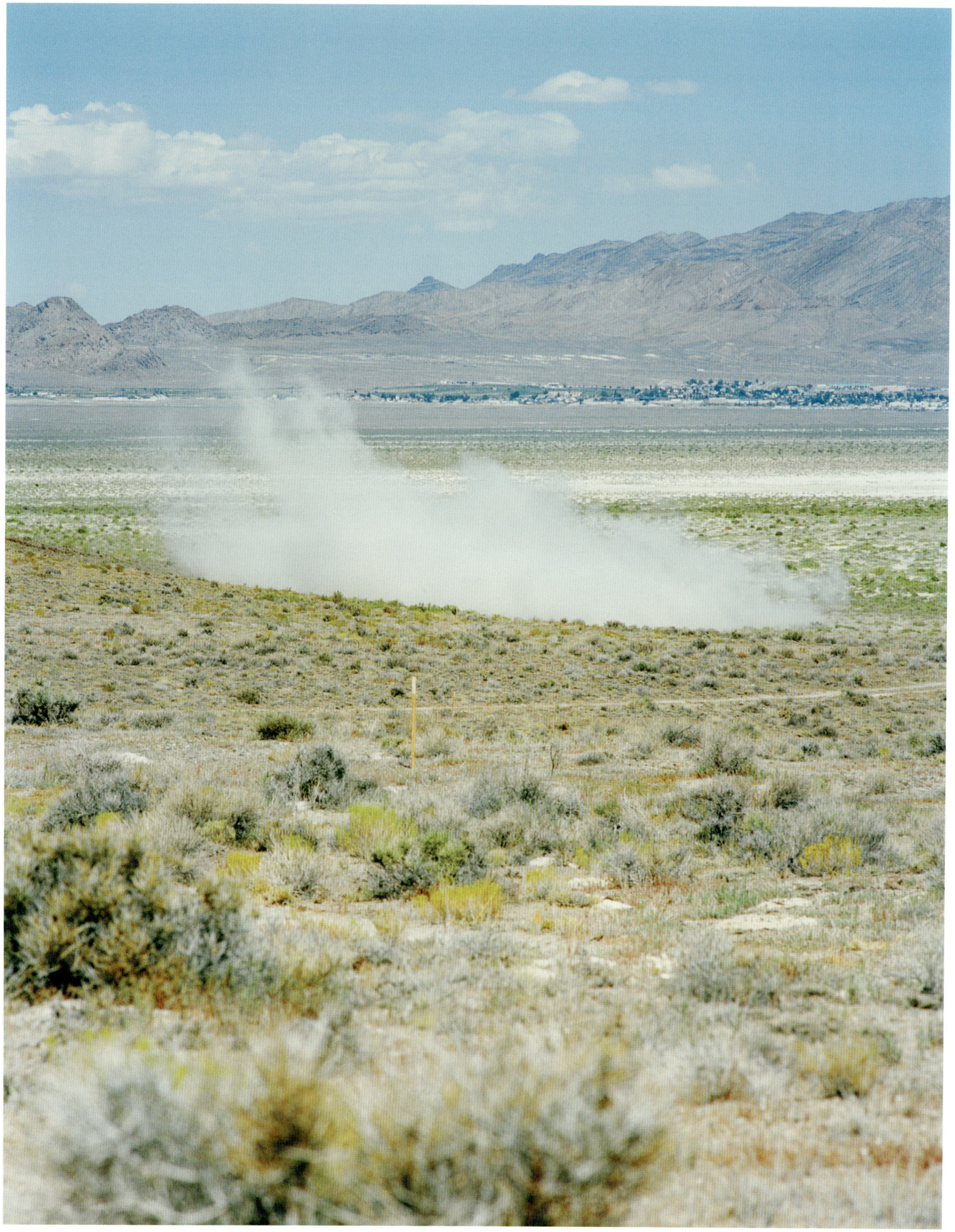

VI. CASINO

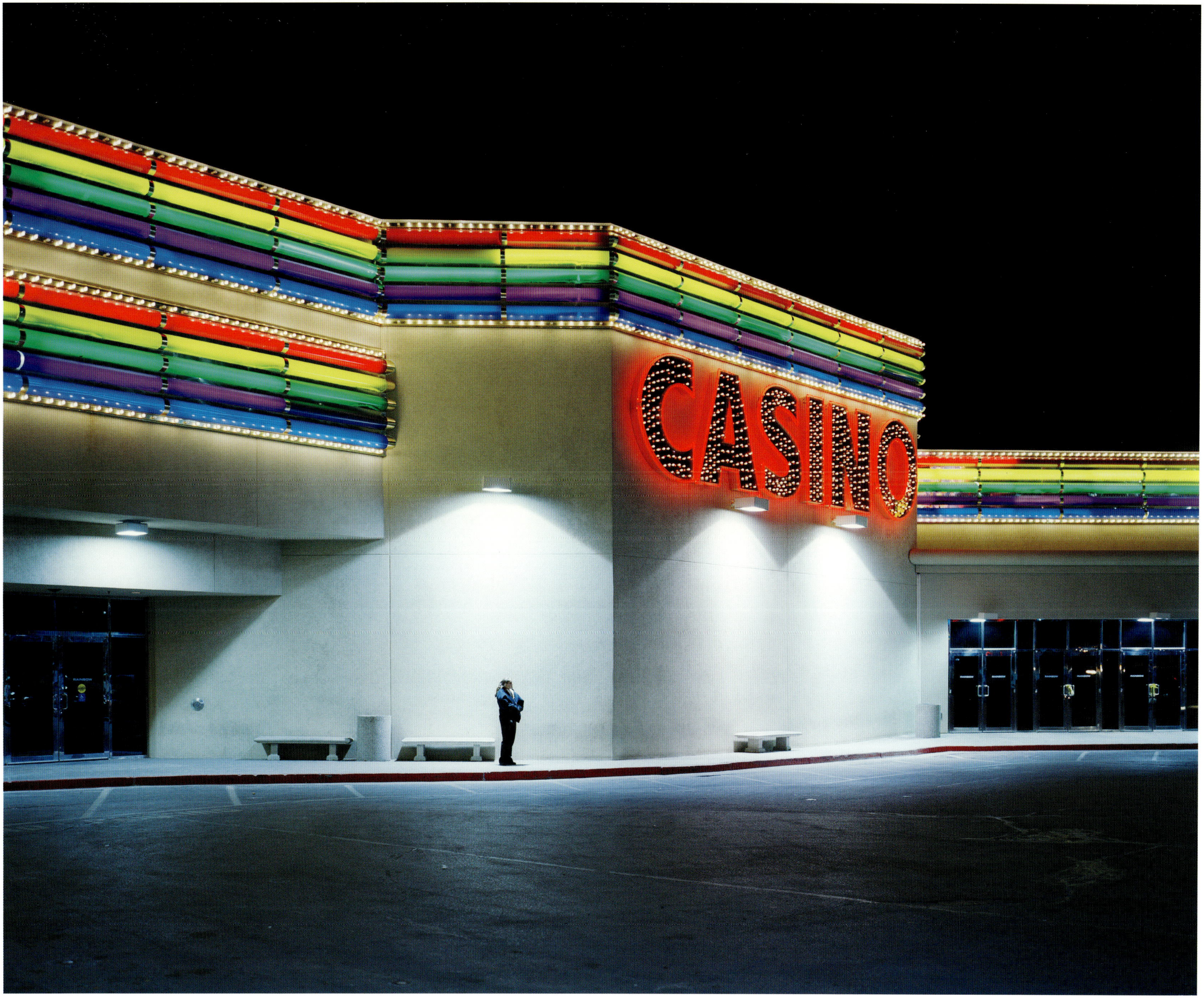
CASINO

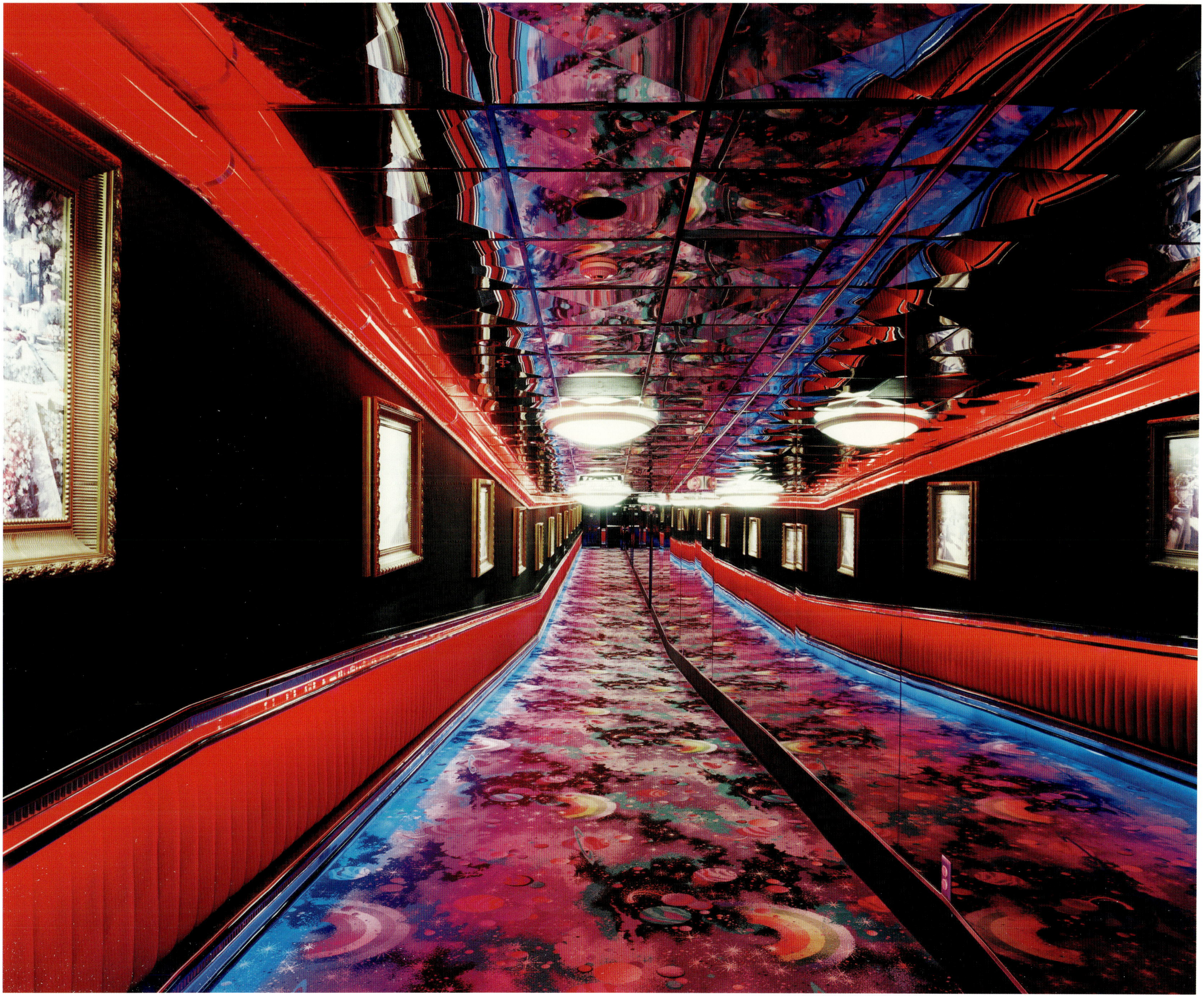

VI.3

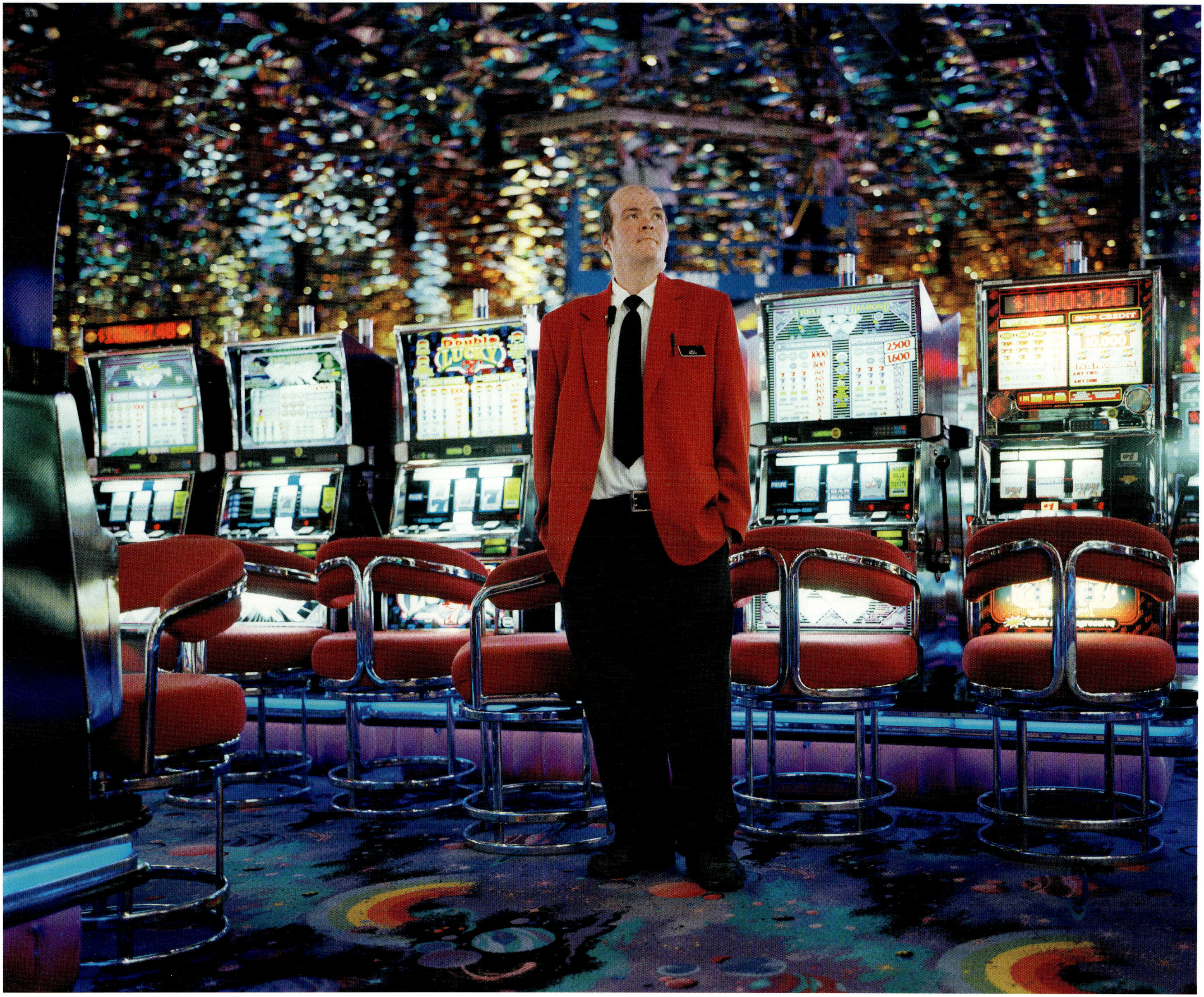
Double LUCKY
2500
1600

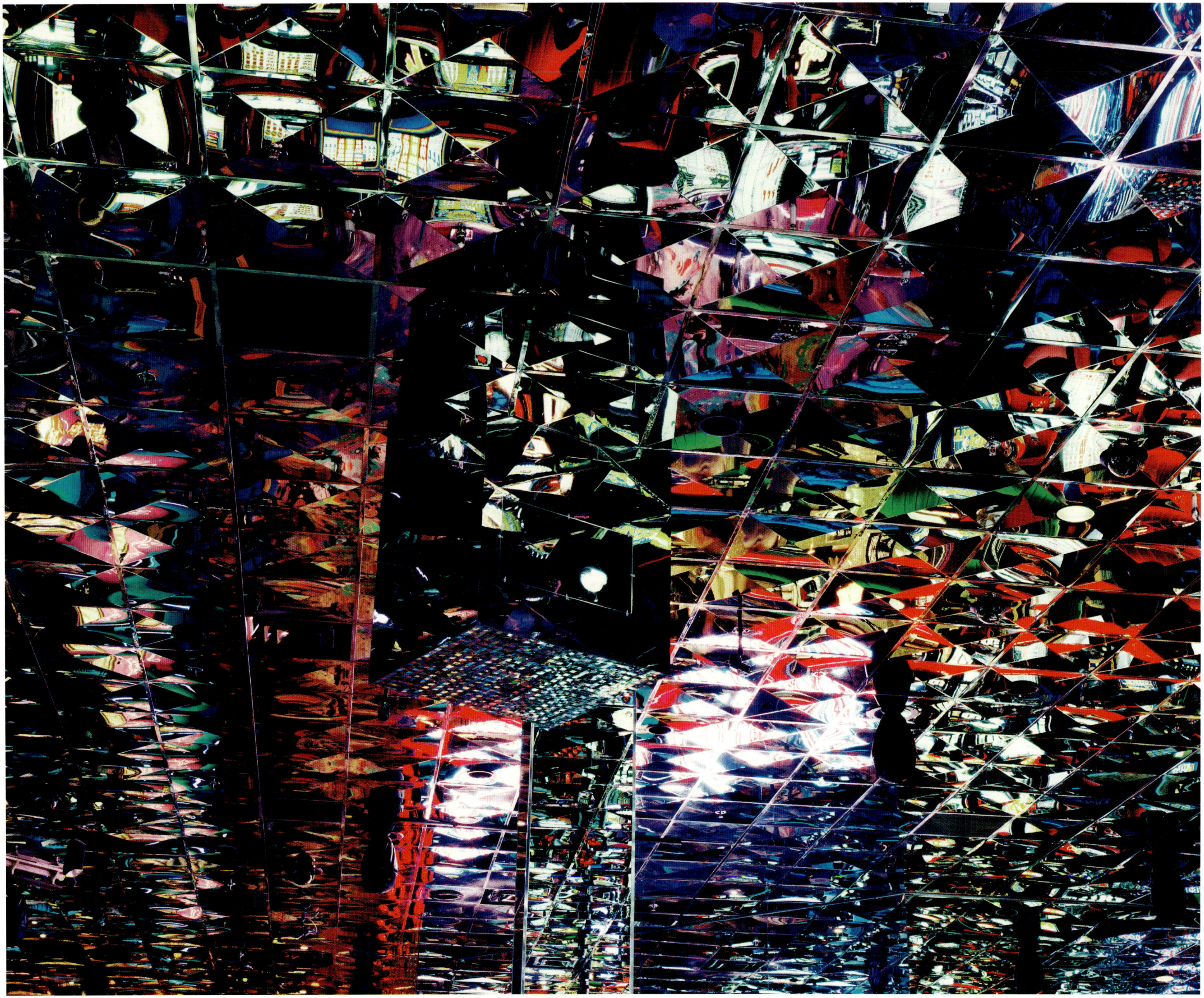

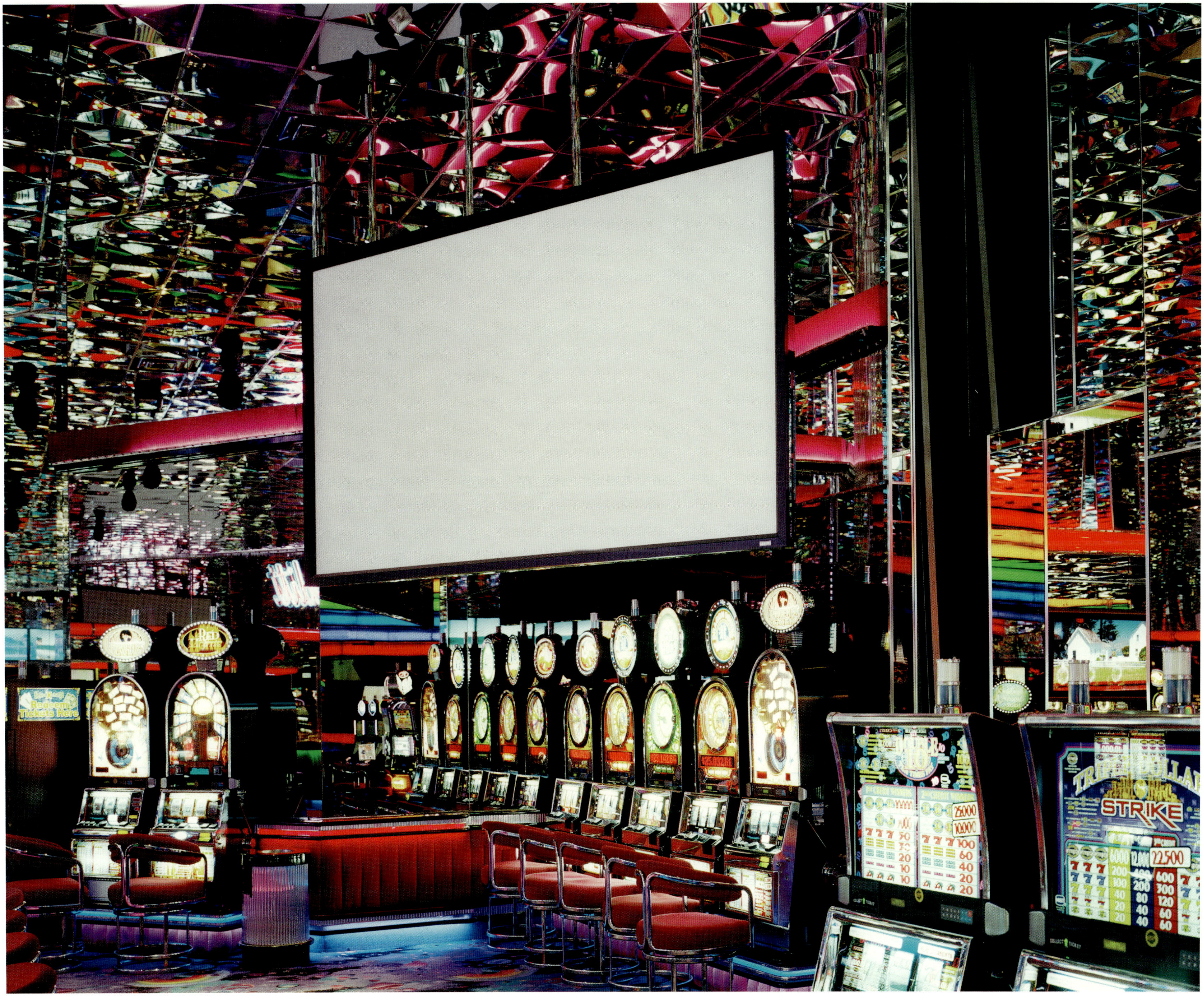
STRIKE

VI.4, VI.5
VI.6

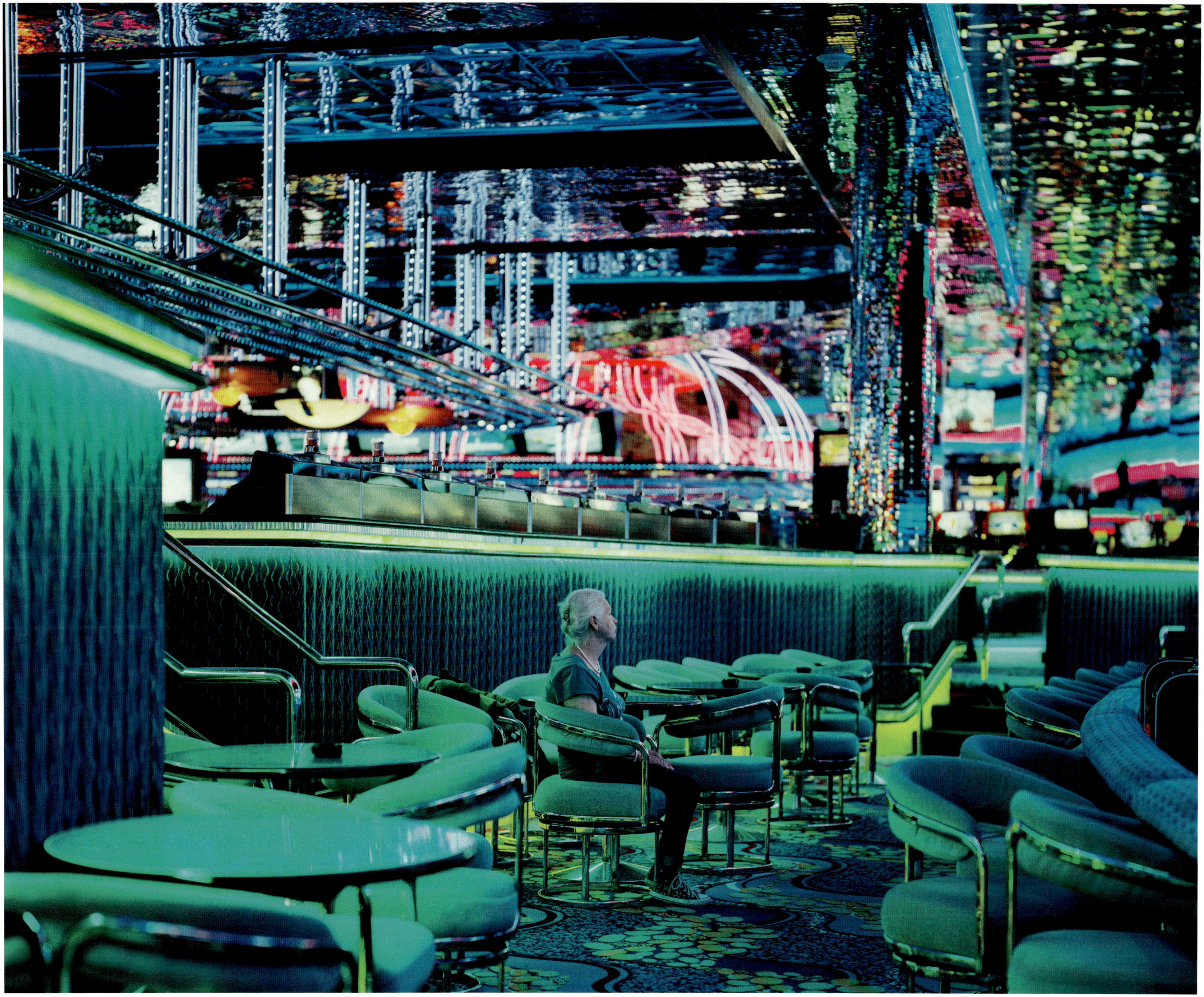

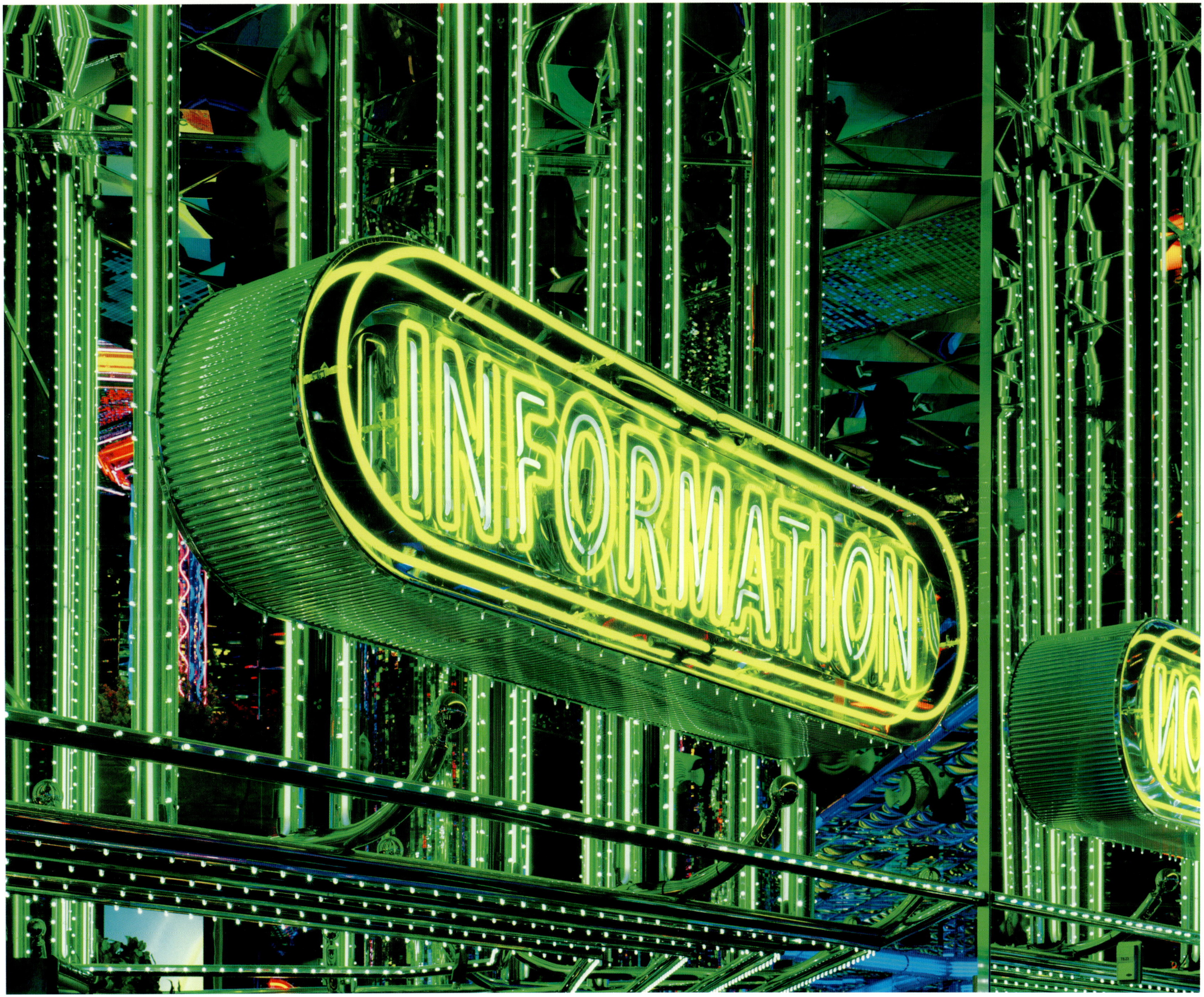
INFORMATION

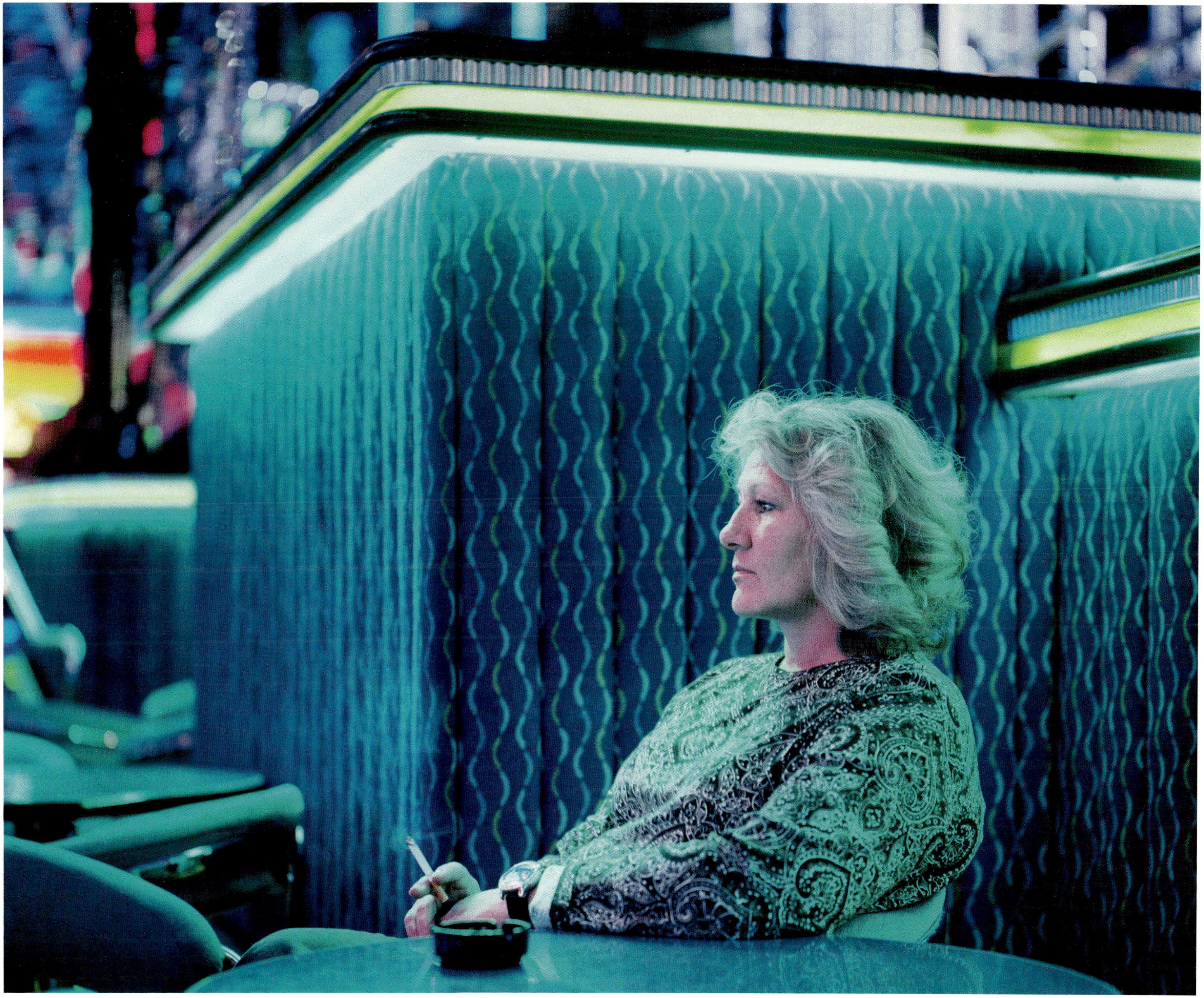

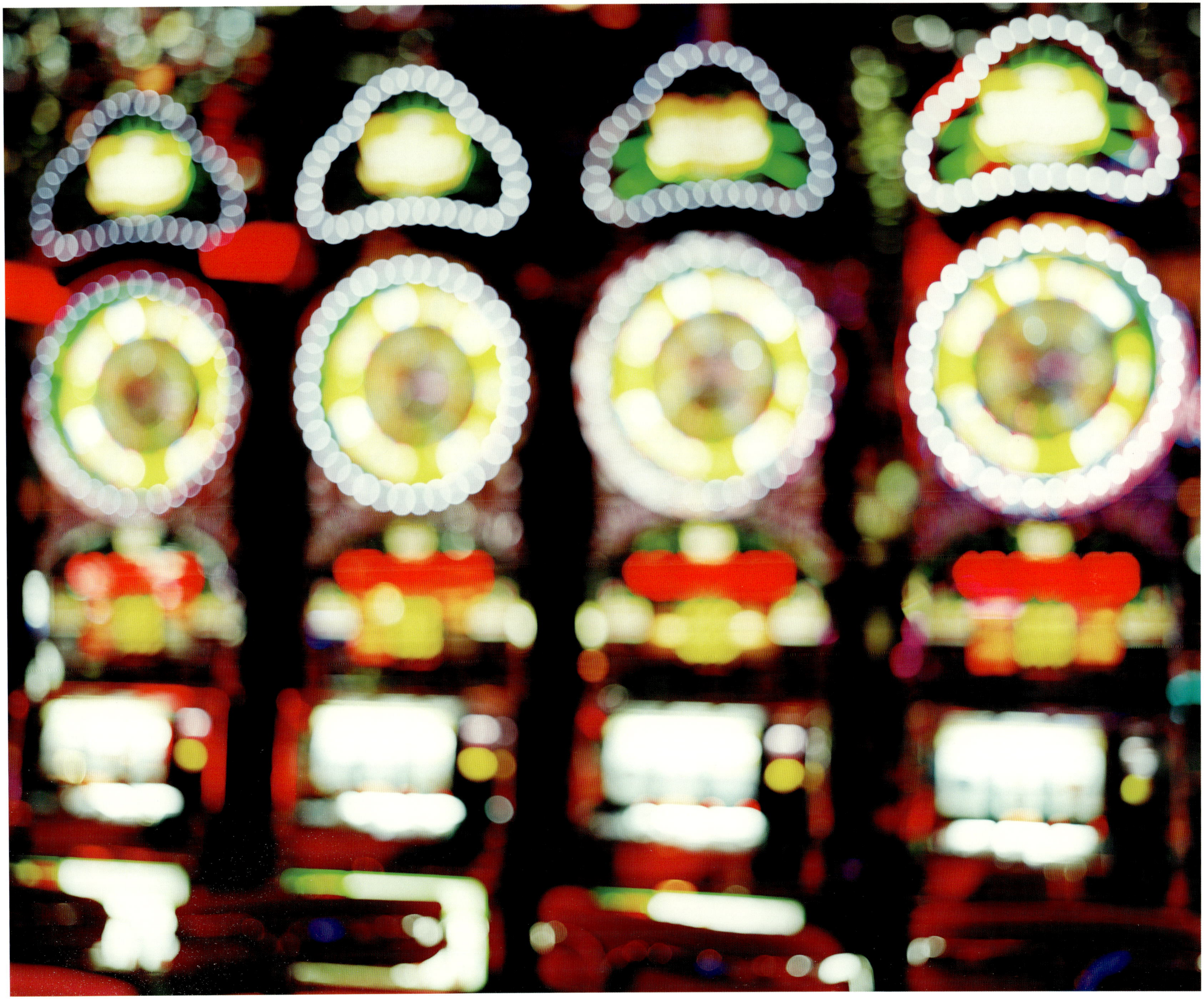

VII. BONNEVILLE

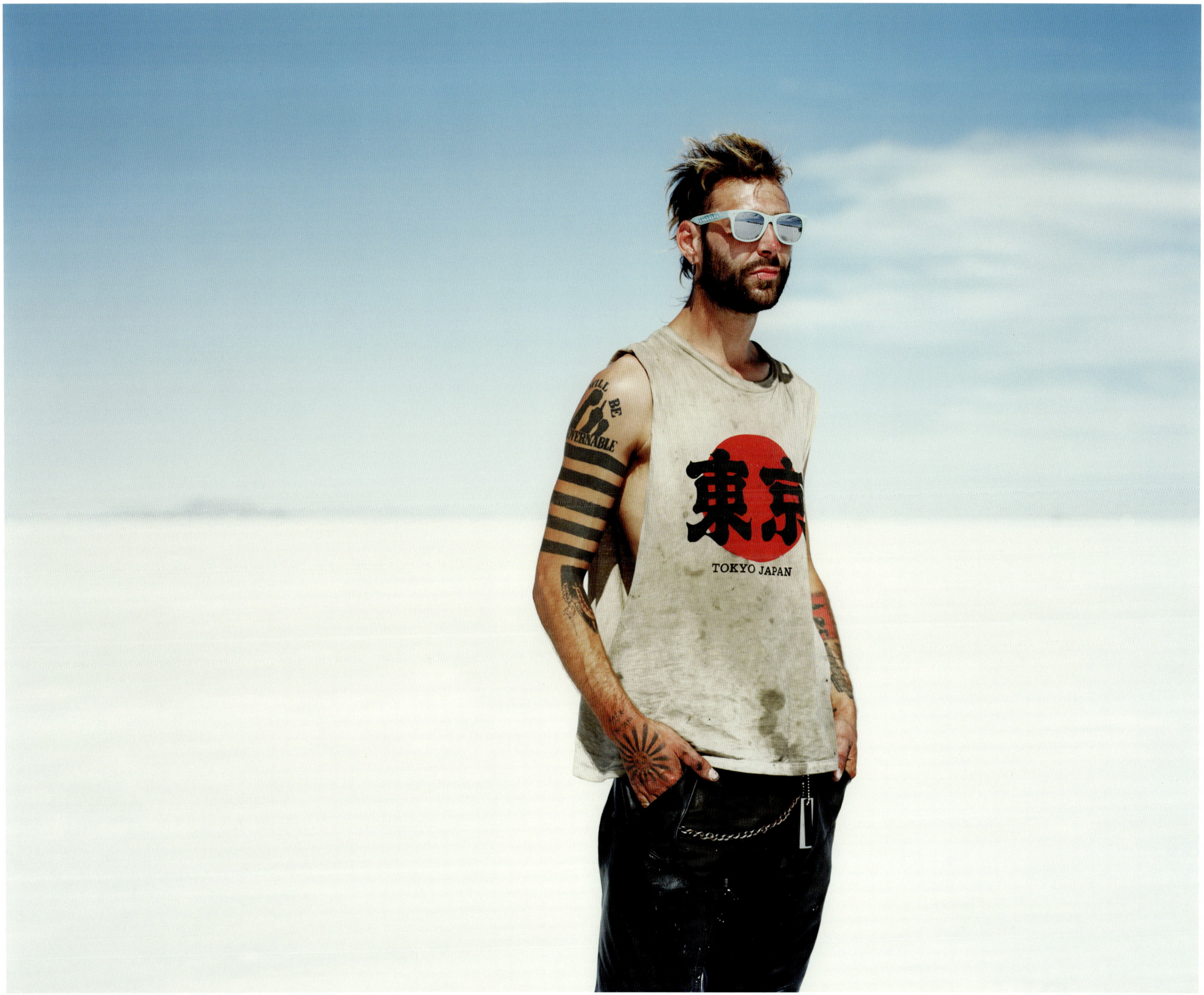
東京
TOKYO JAPAN

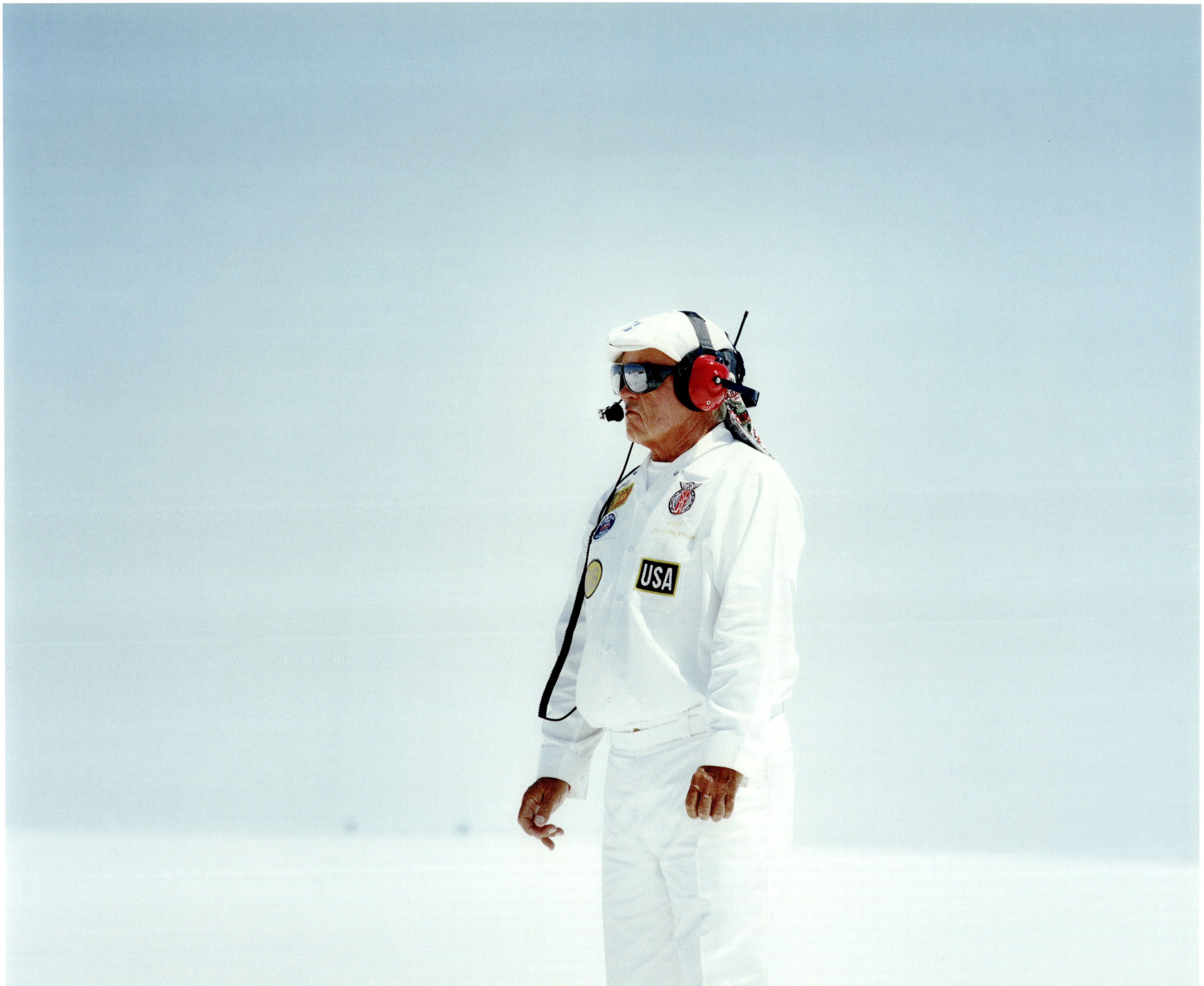
USA

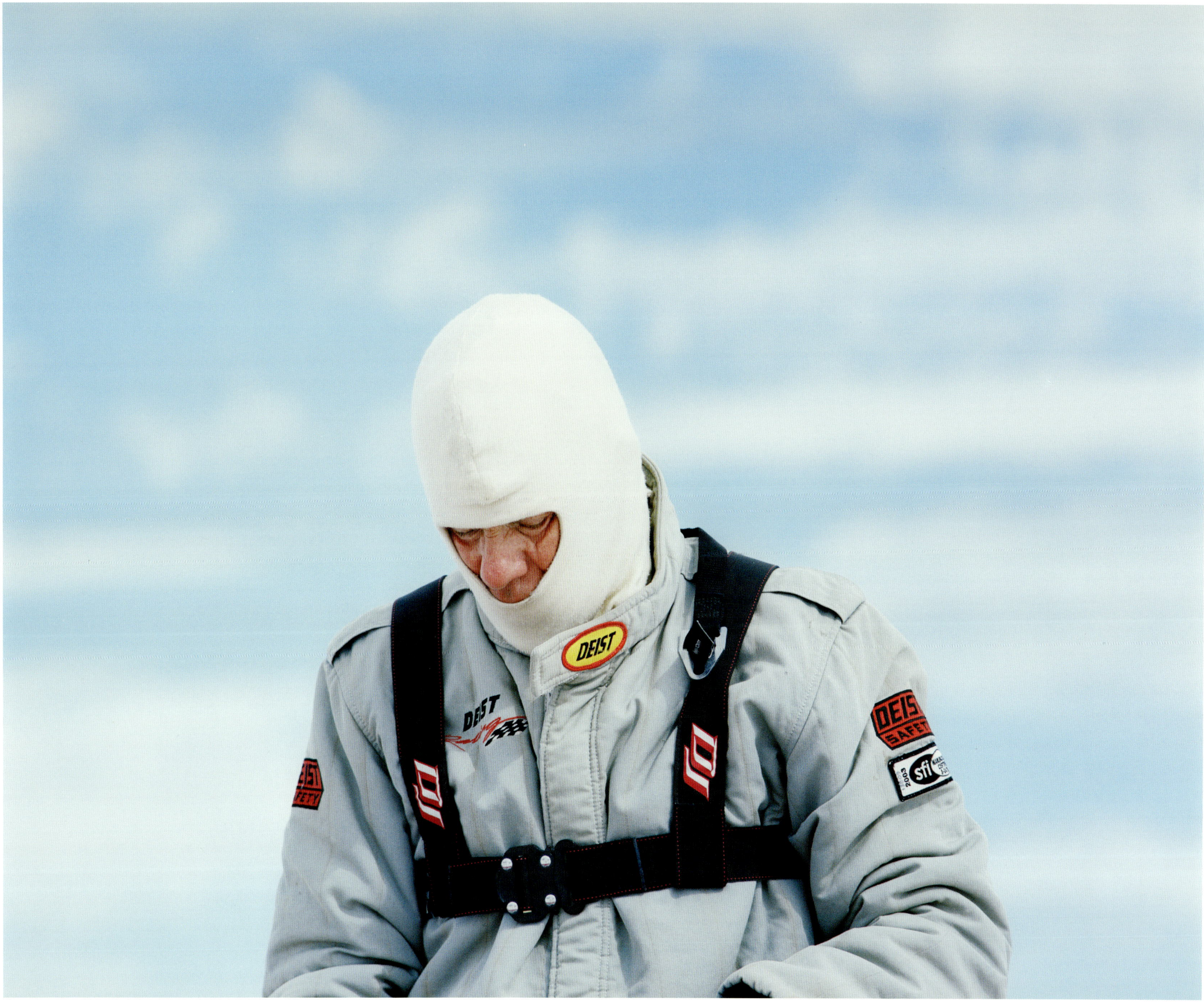
DEIST
DEIST
sfi
2003

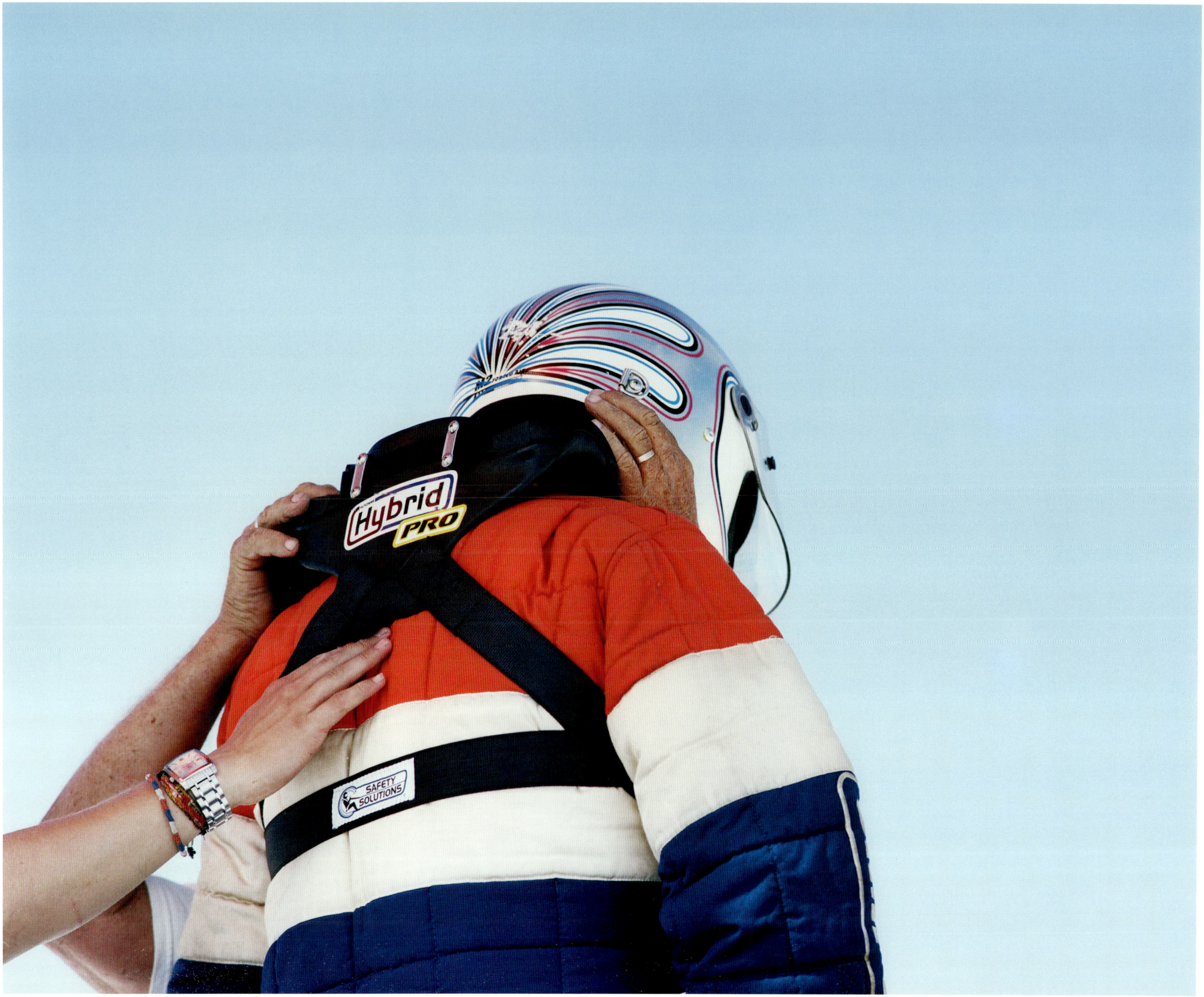
Hybrid
PRO
SAFETY
SOLUTIONS

VIII. VERTELLUS

VIII.1

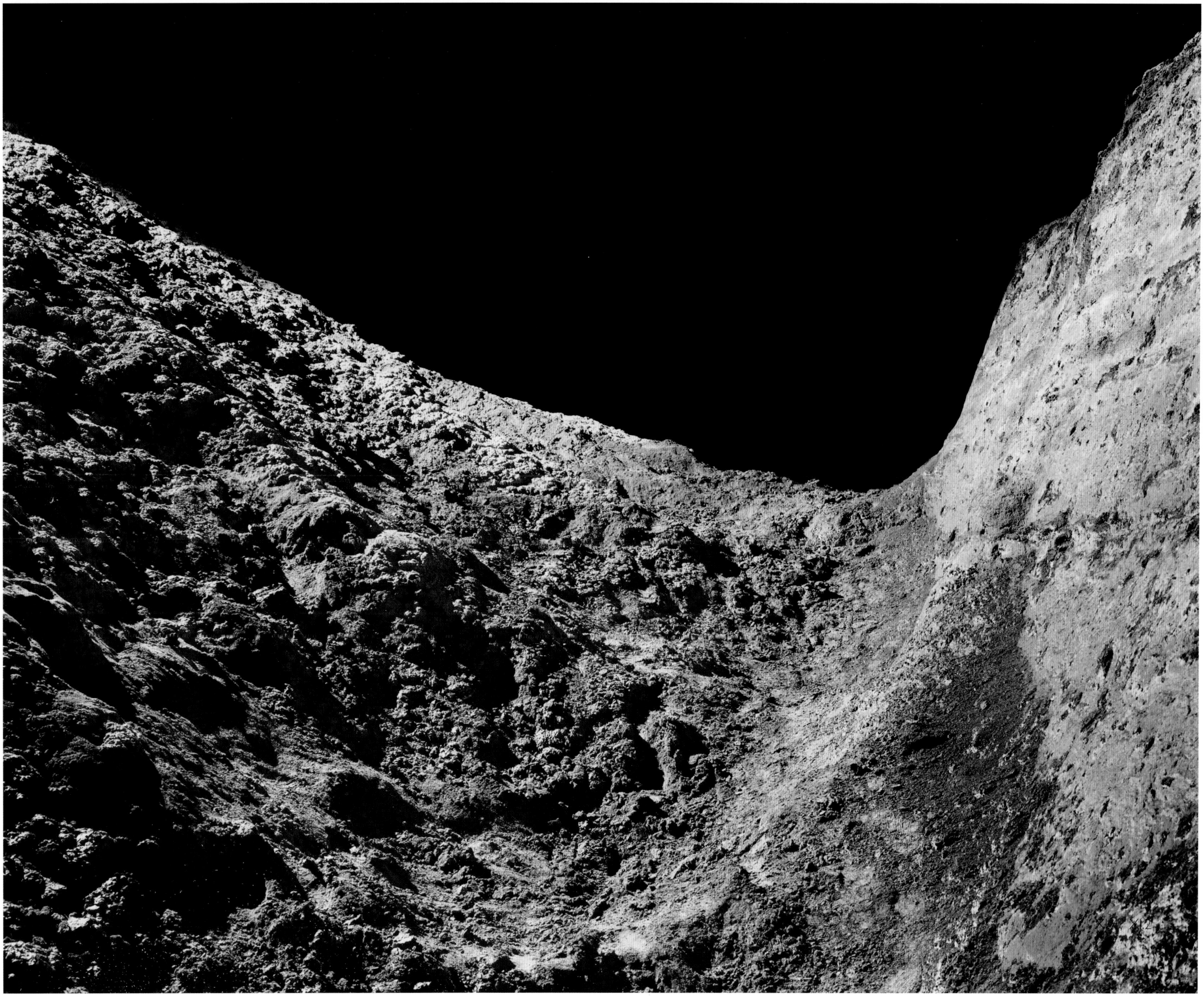

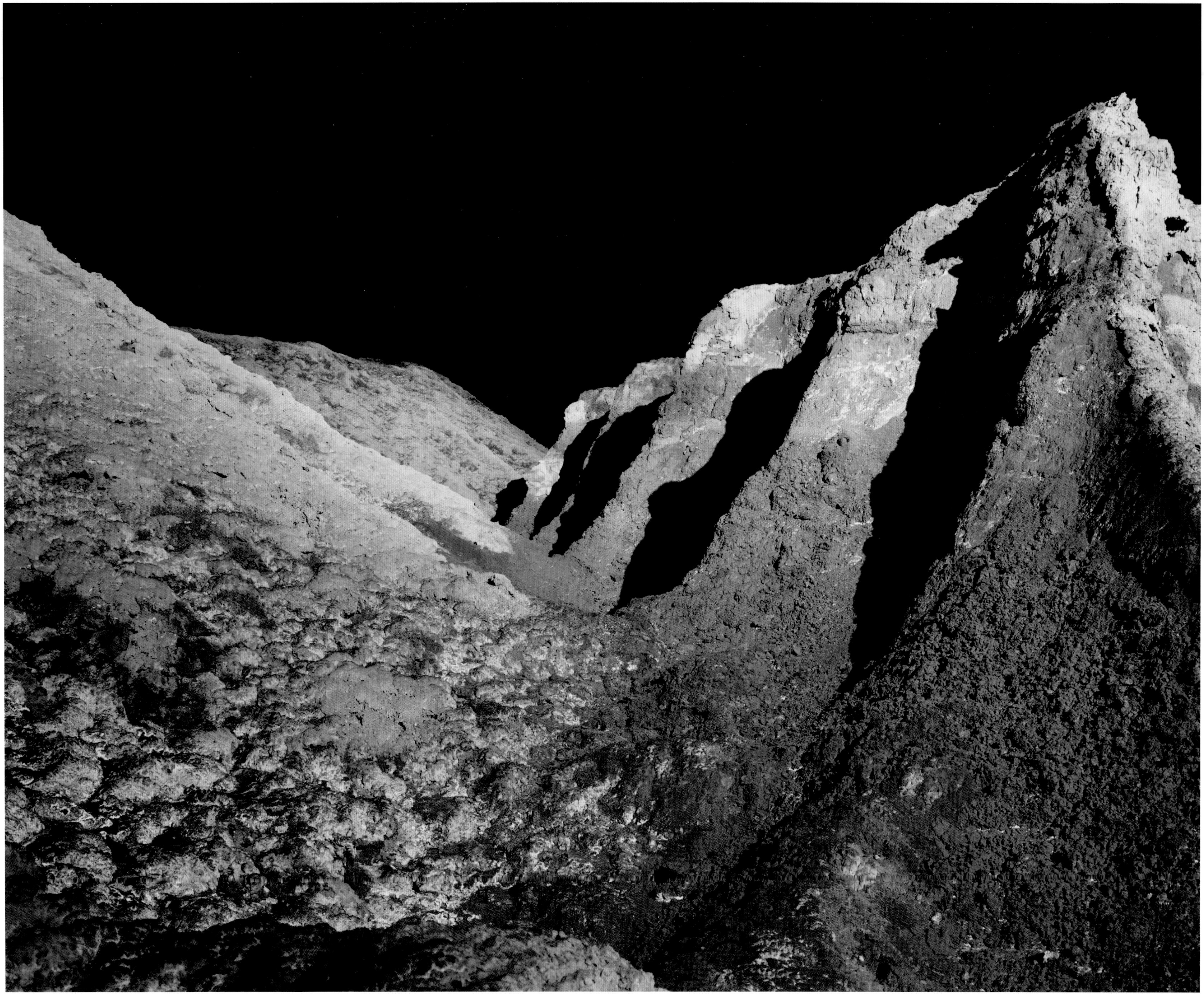

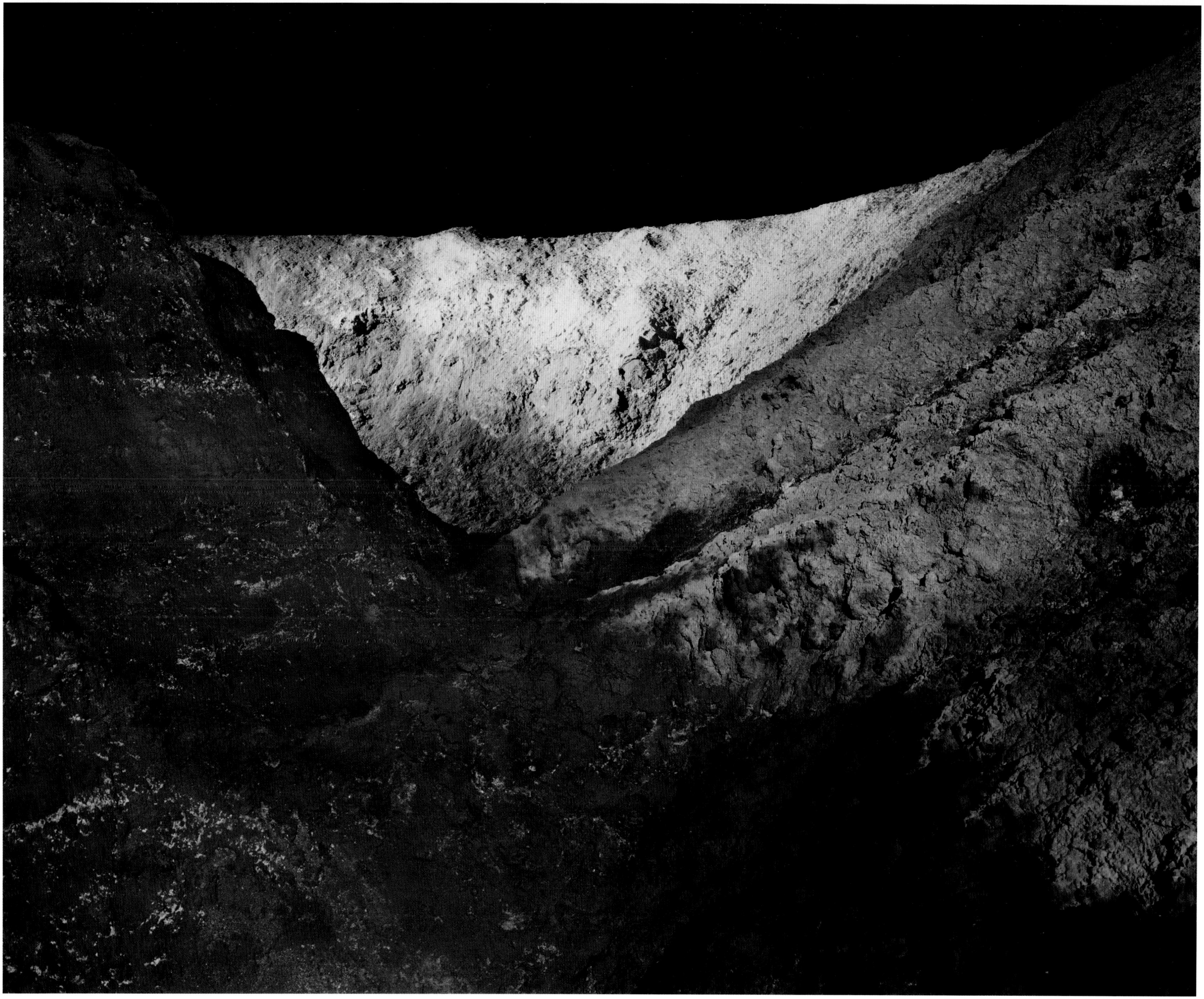

VIII.2, VIII.3
VIII.4

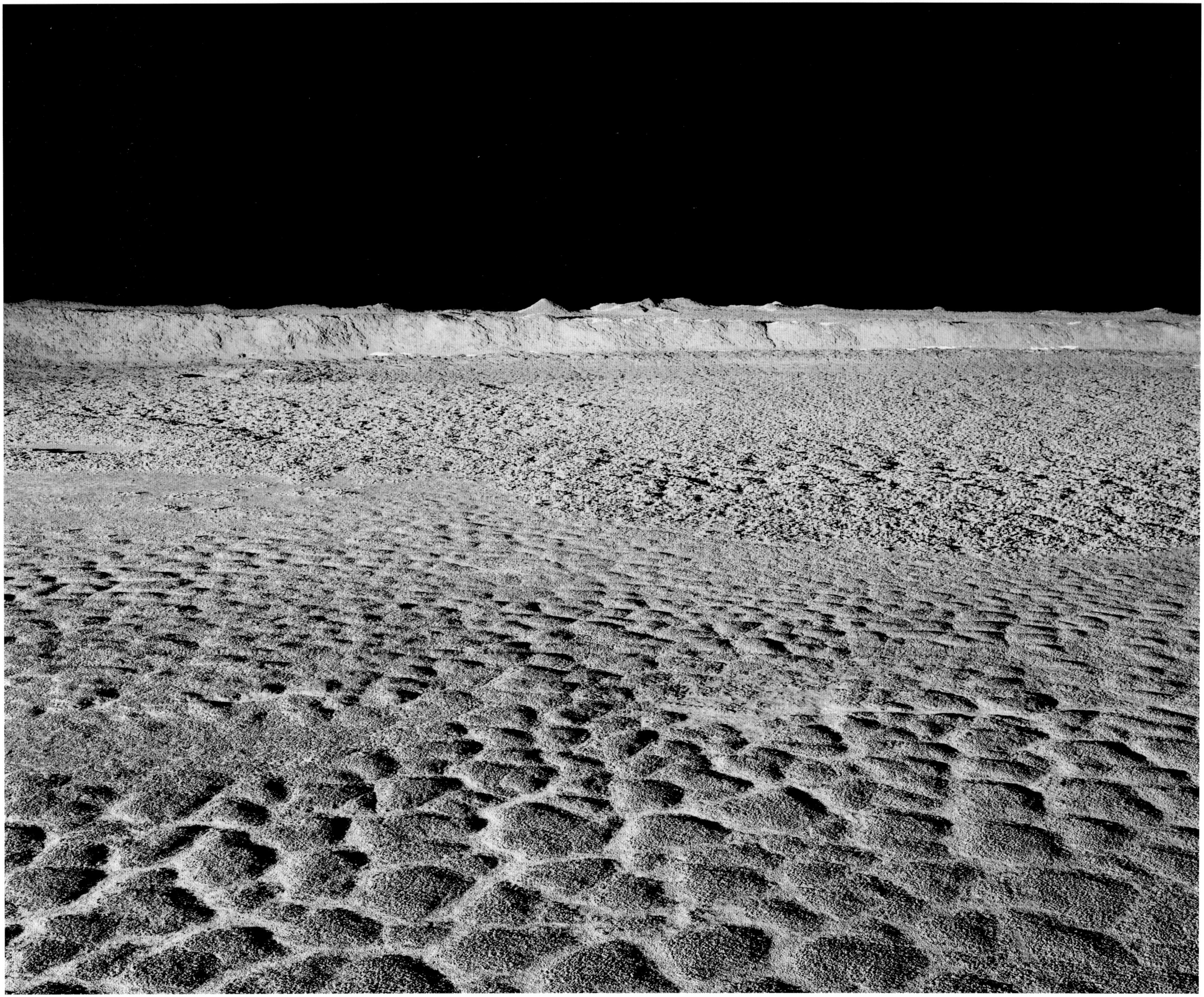

VIII.5

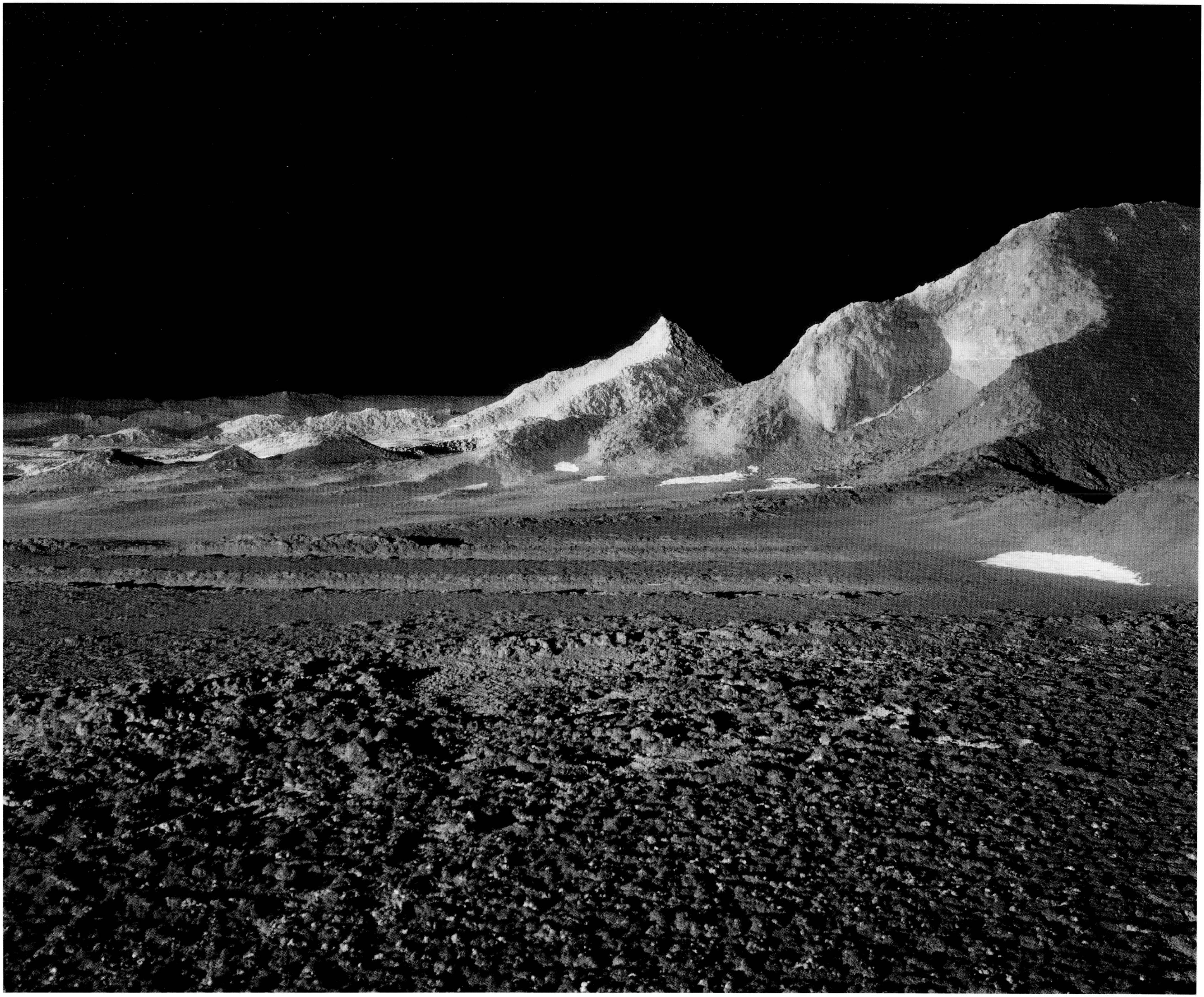

IX. REST AREA

IX.1

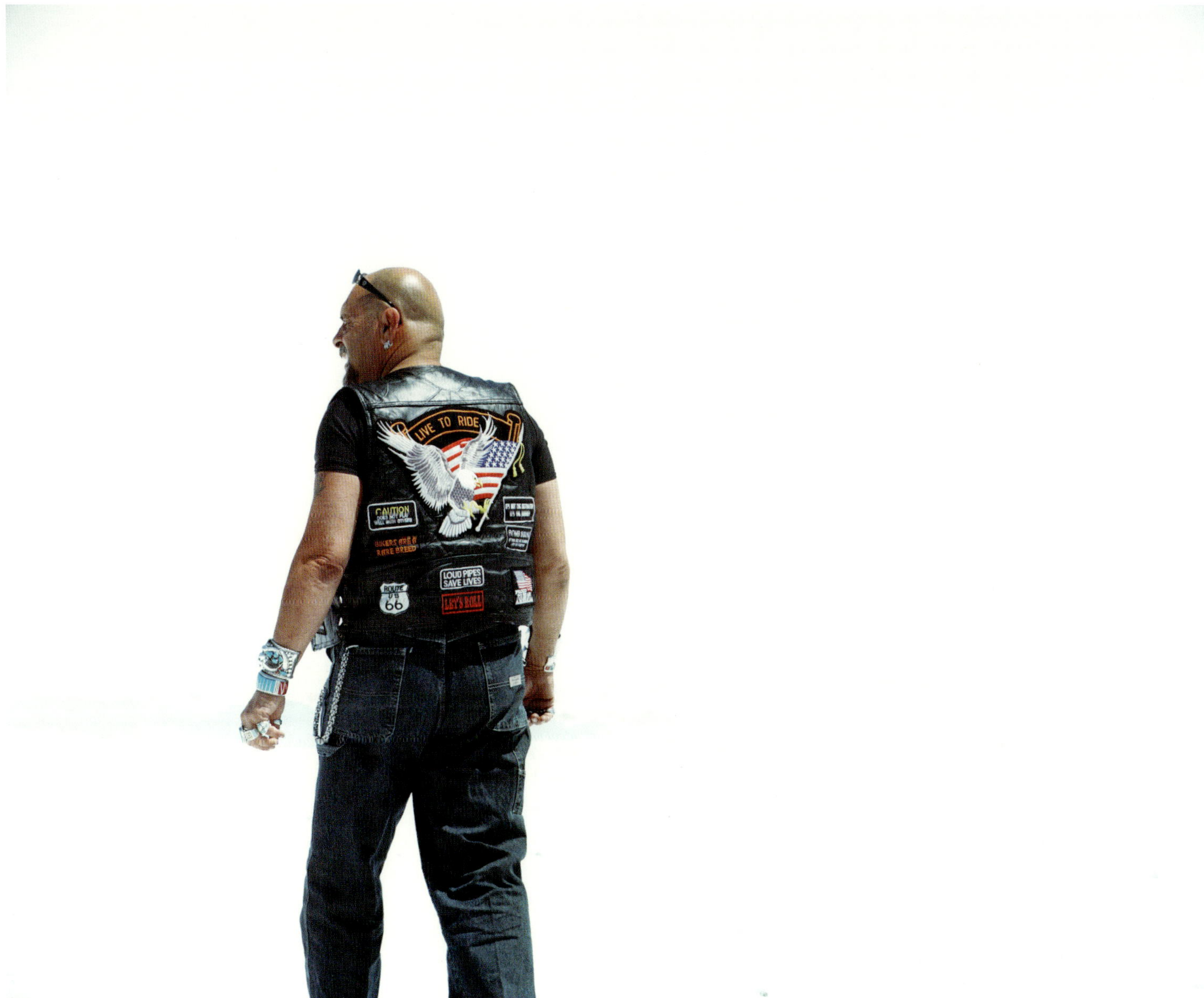
LIVE TO RIDE
CAUTION
LOUD PIPES
SAVE LIVES
LET'S ROLL
66

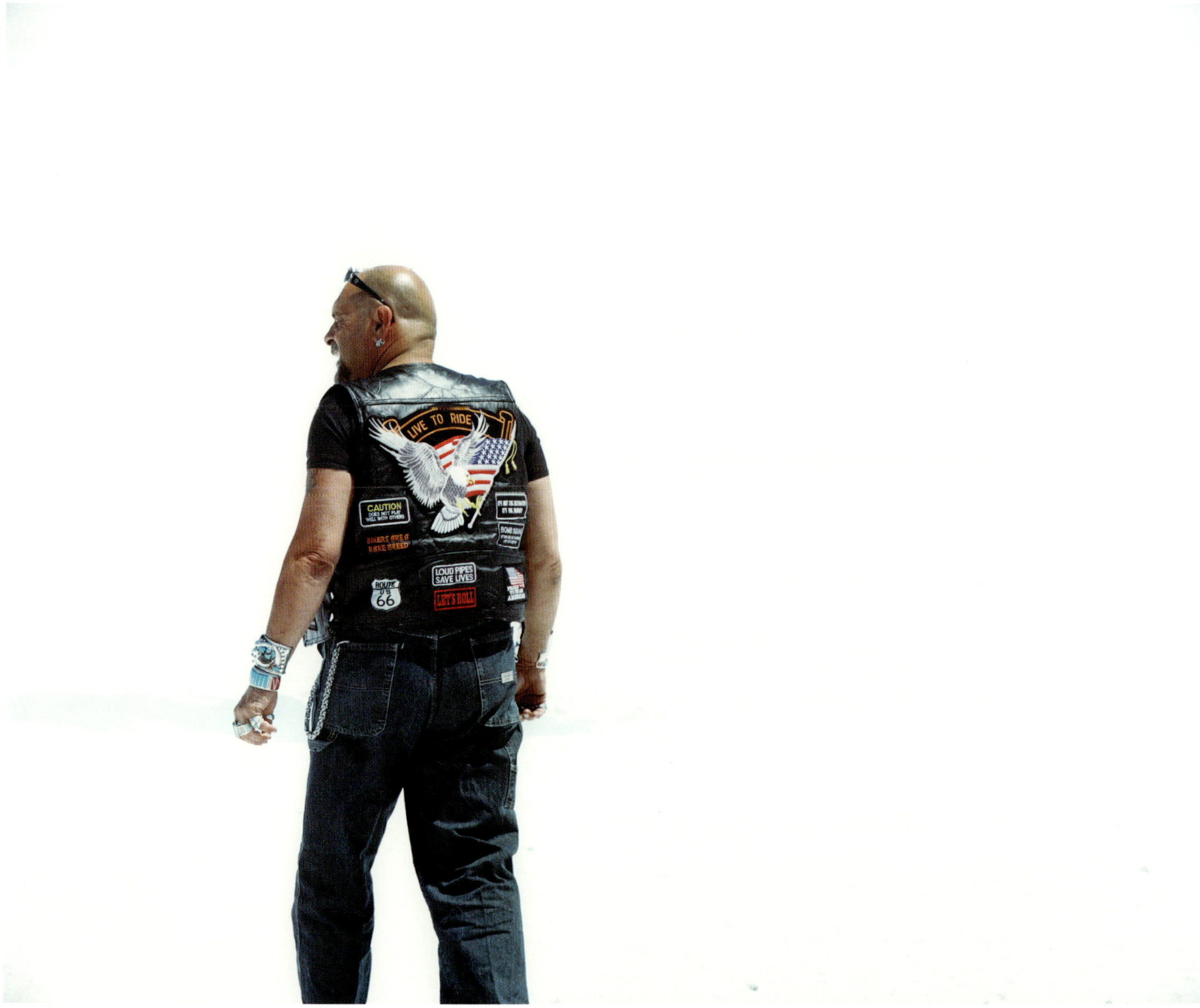
LIVE TO RIDE
CAUTION
LOUD PIPES
SAVE LIVES
ROUTE
66
LET'S ROLL

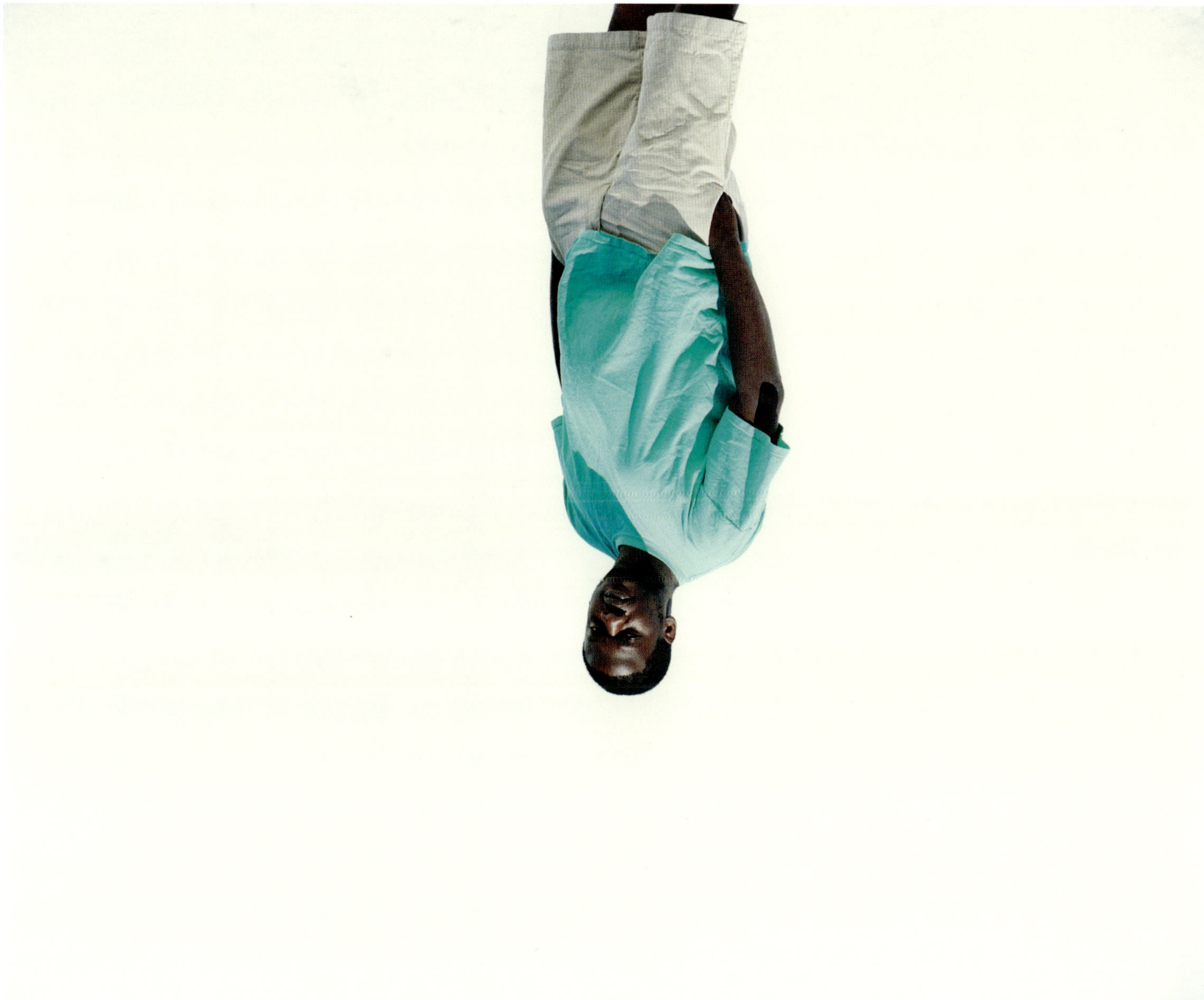

IX.3

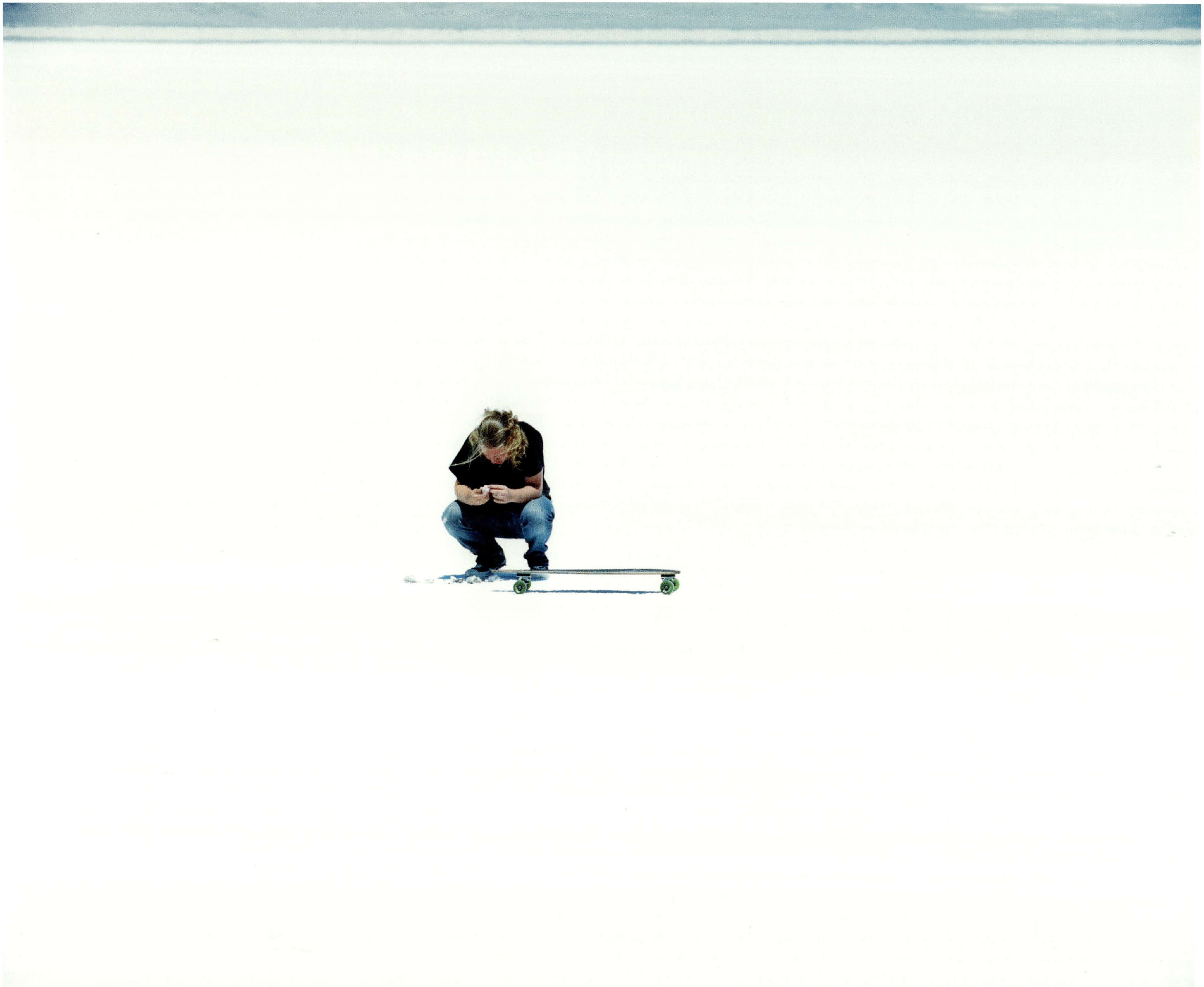

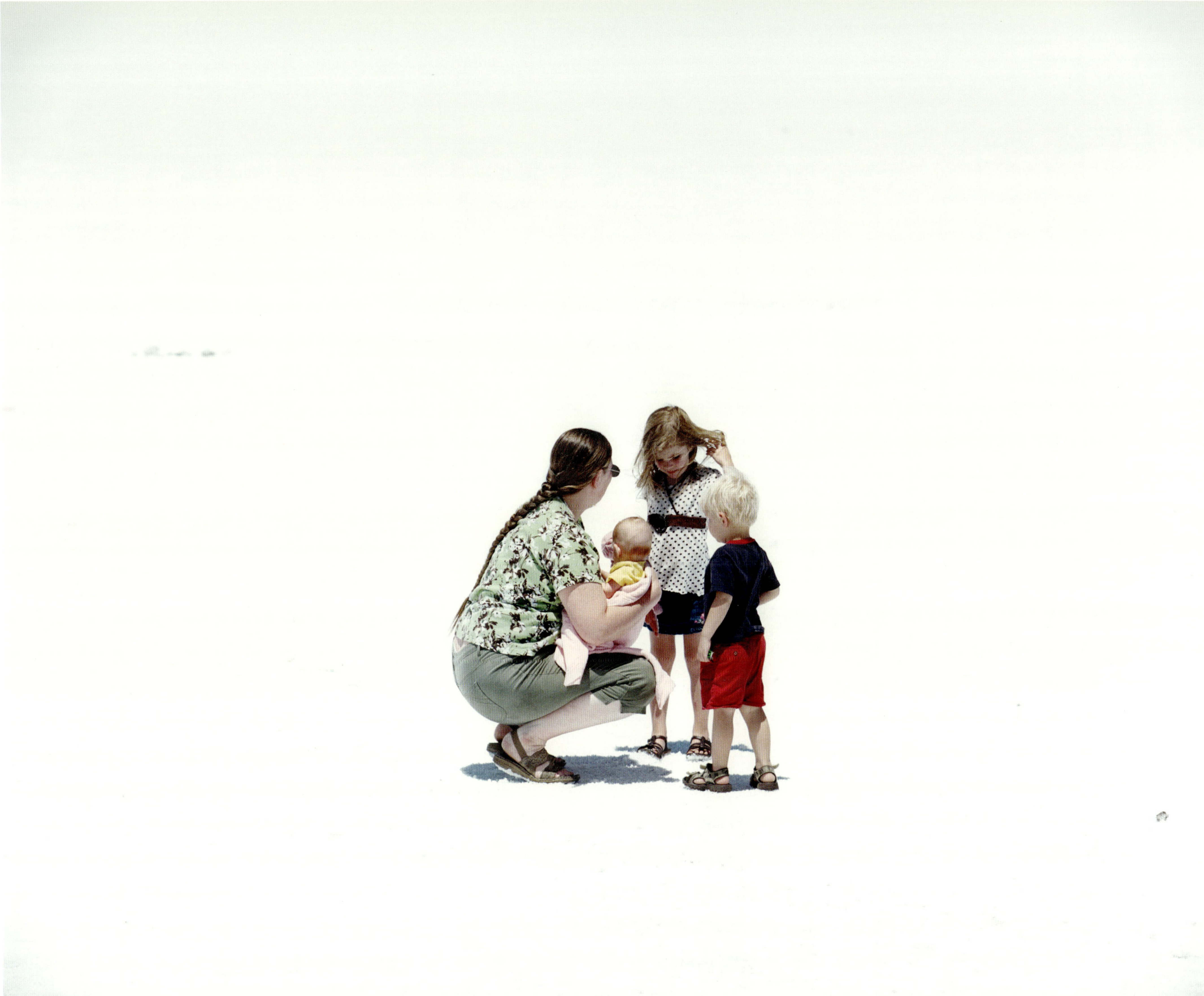

X. NUGGET T748

X.1

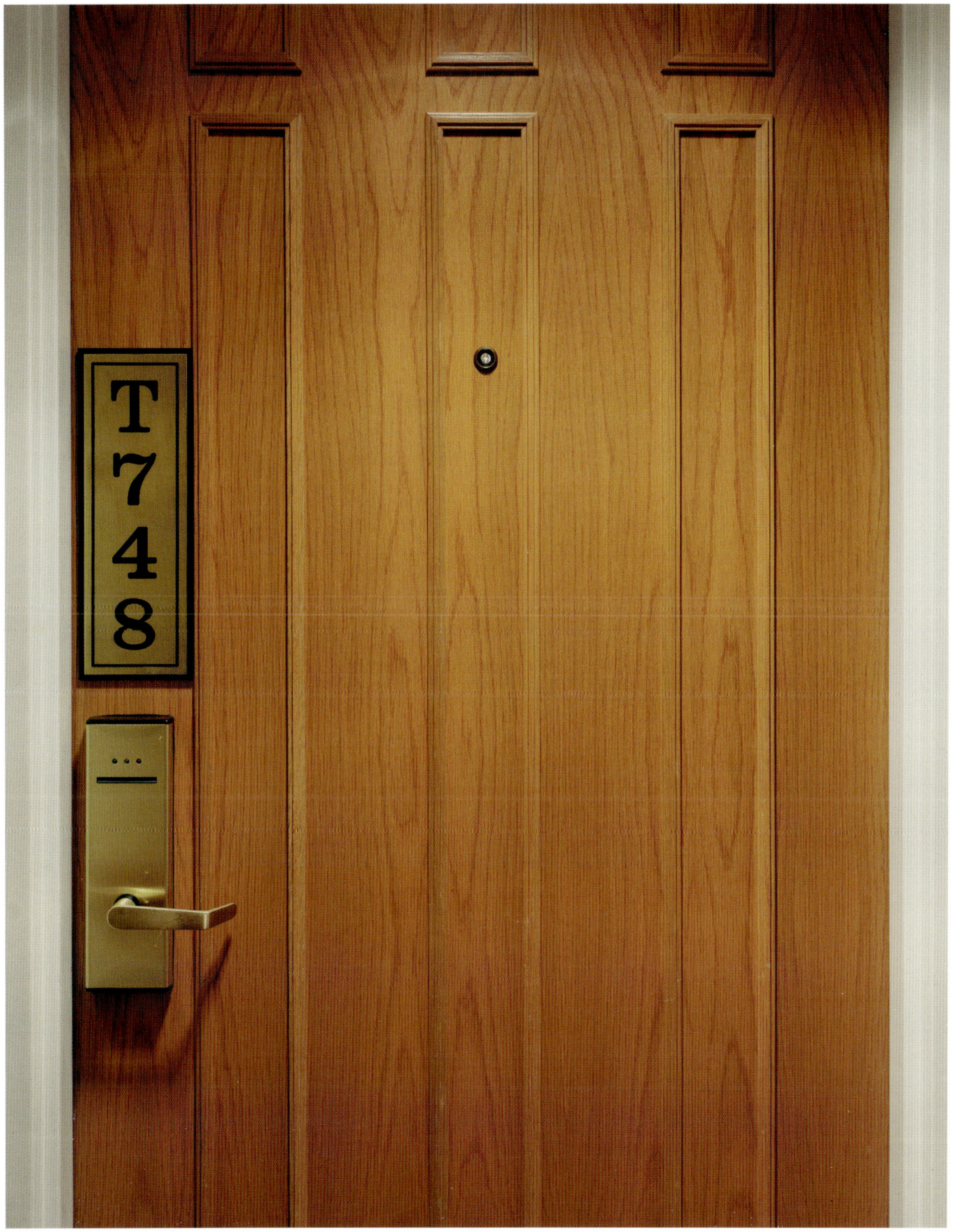
T
7
4
8

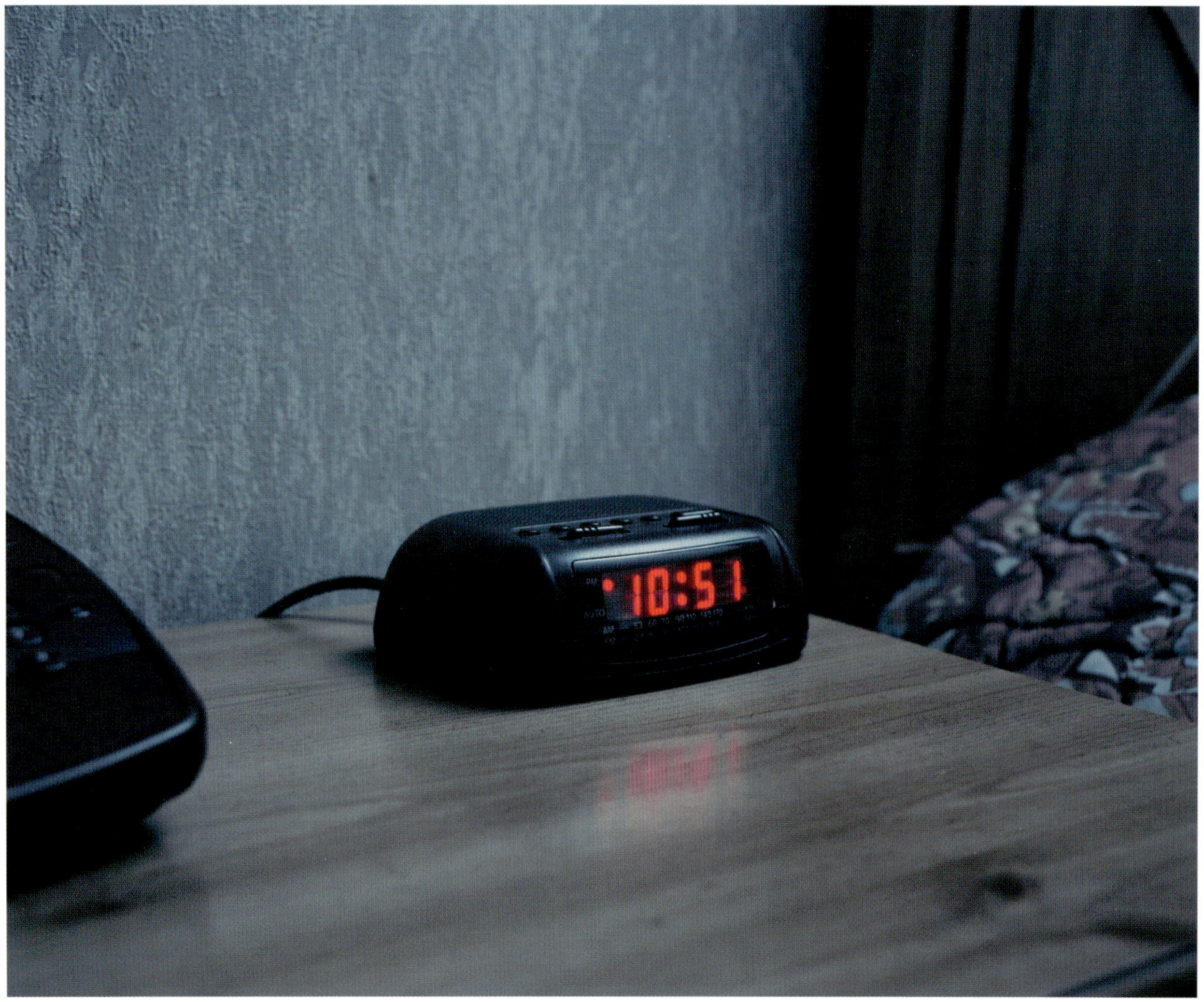

X.2, X.3

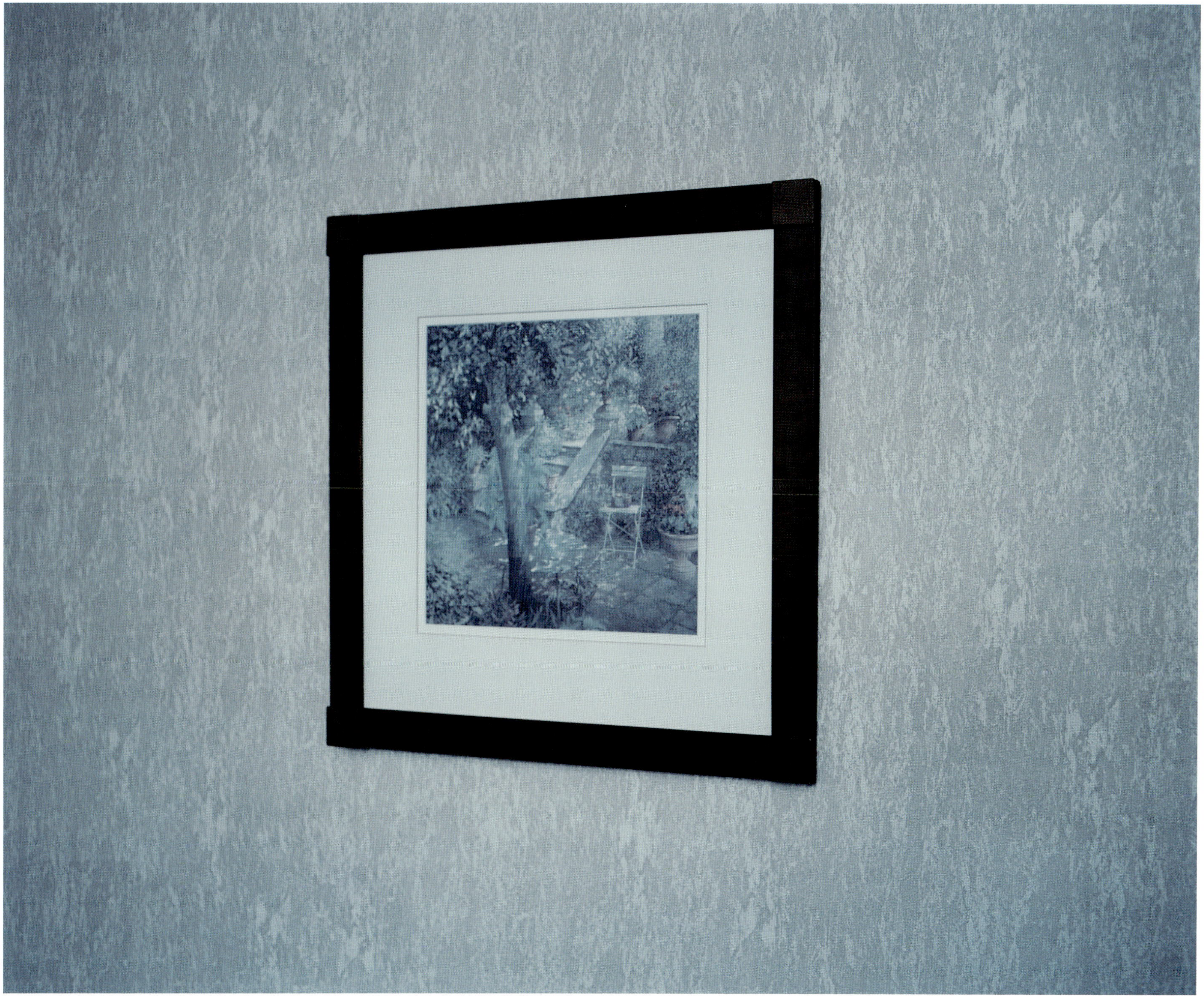

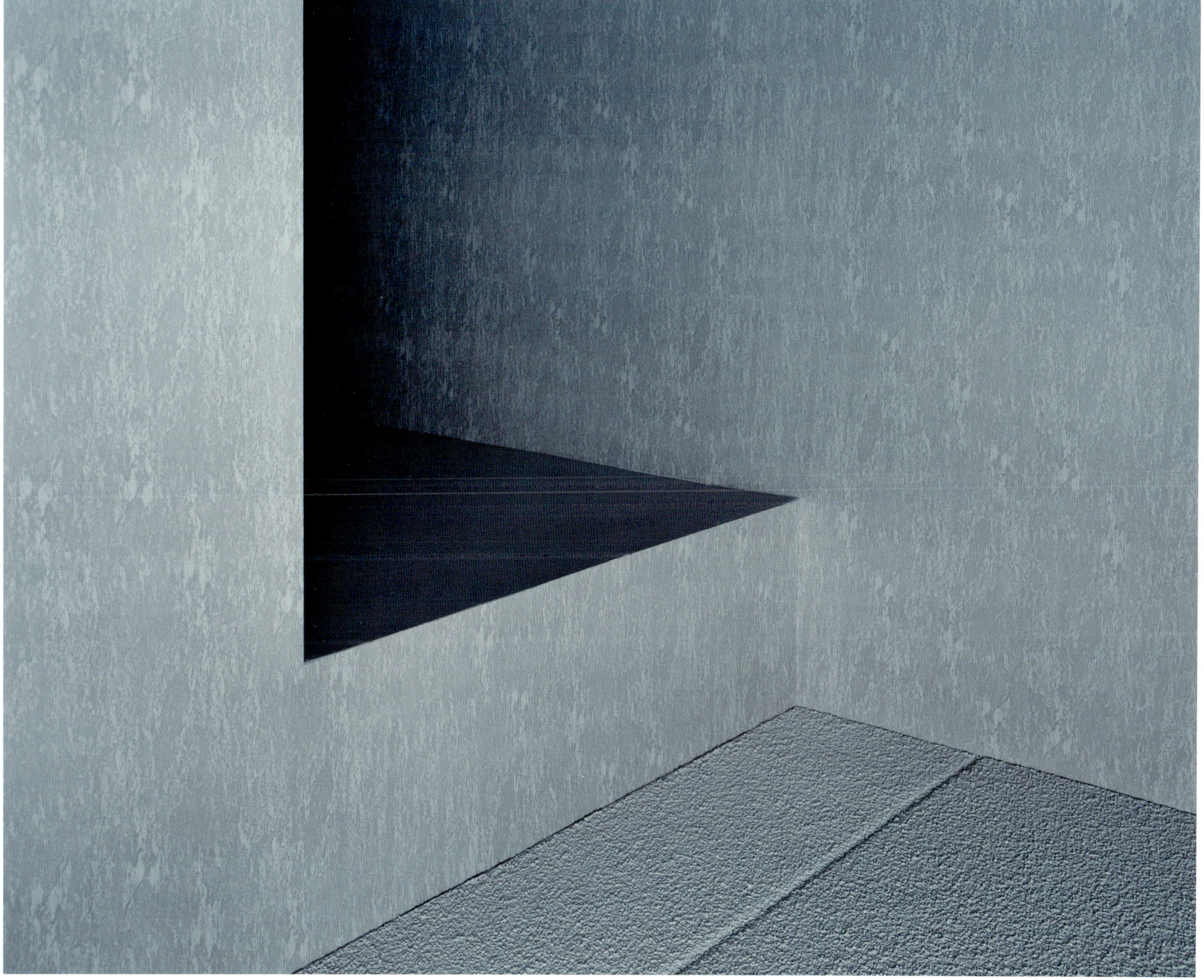

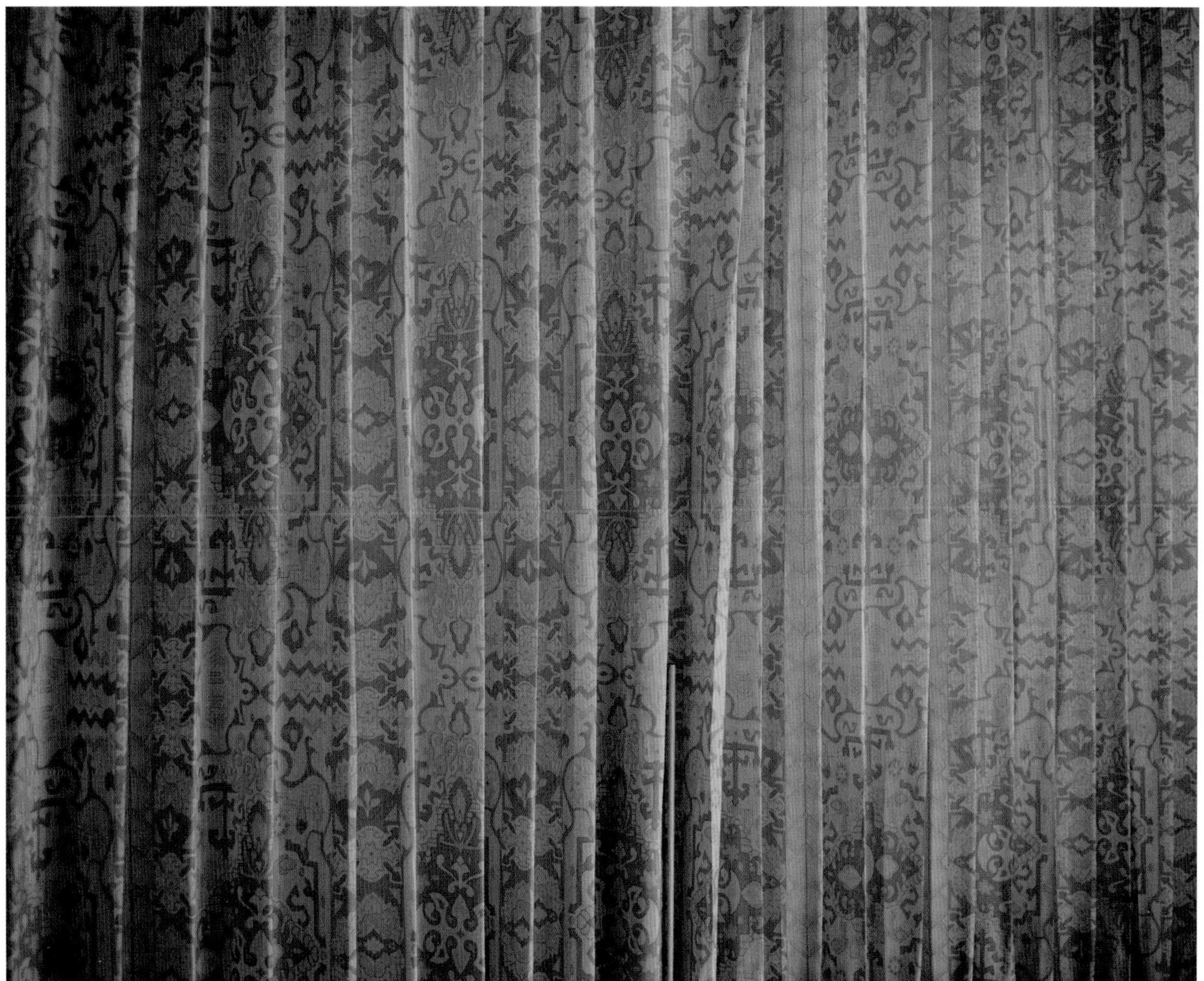

X.6

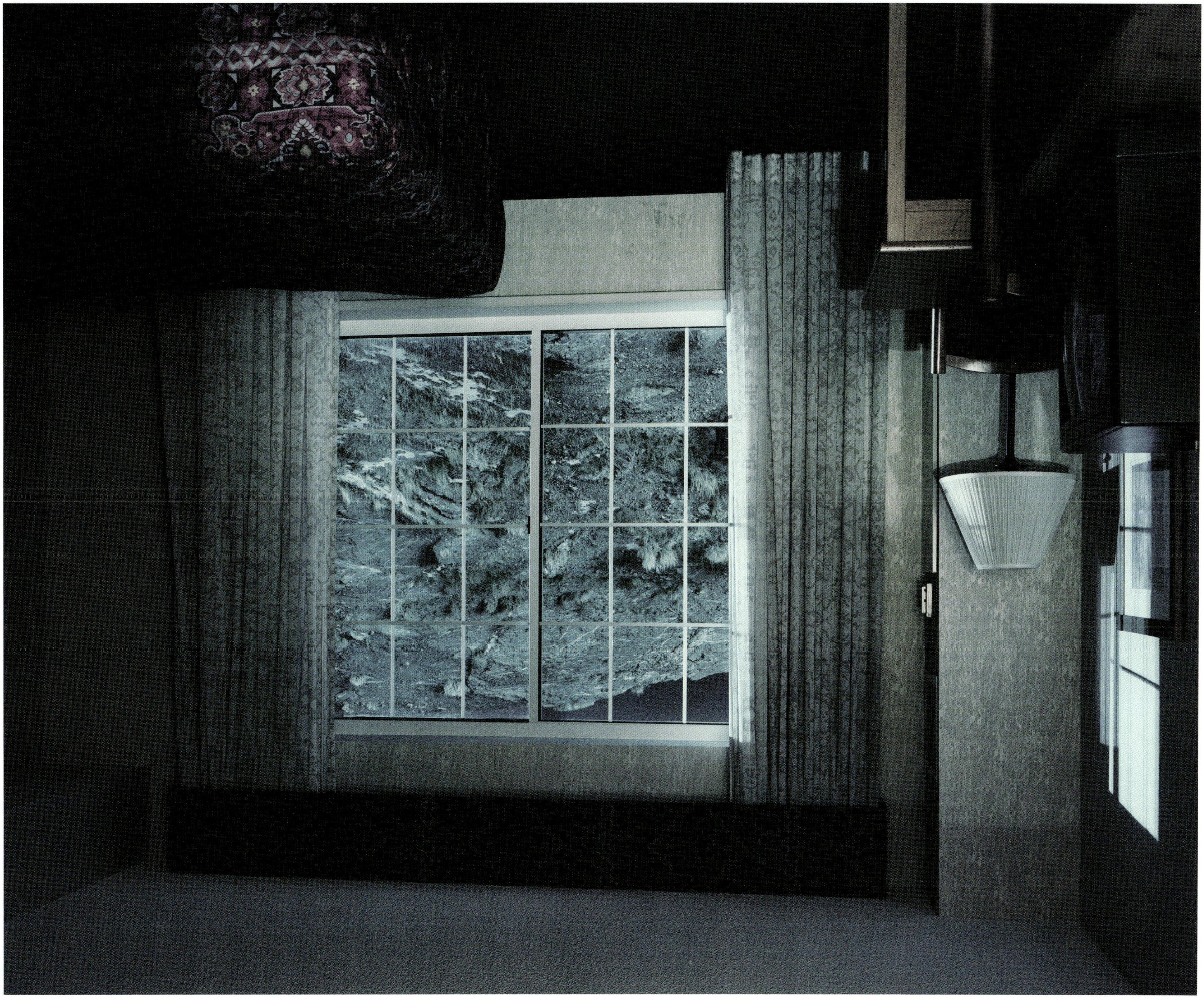

I. FLOATING ISLAND

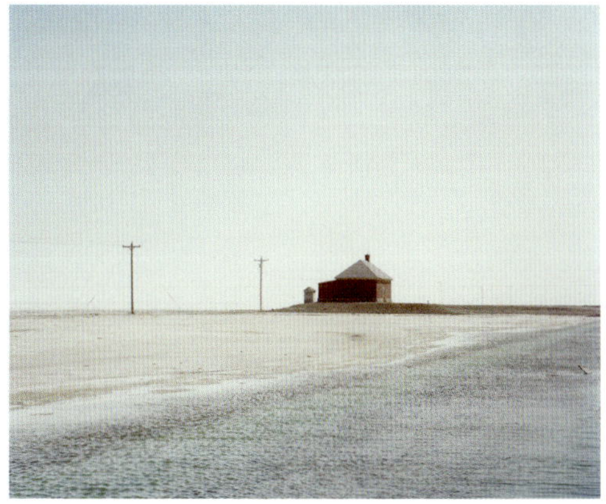

1. Service Building

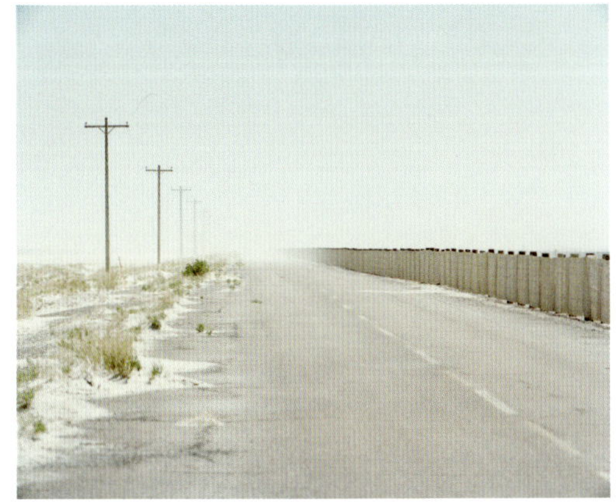

2. Frontage Road I

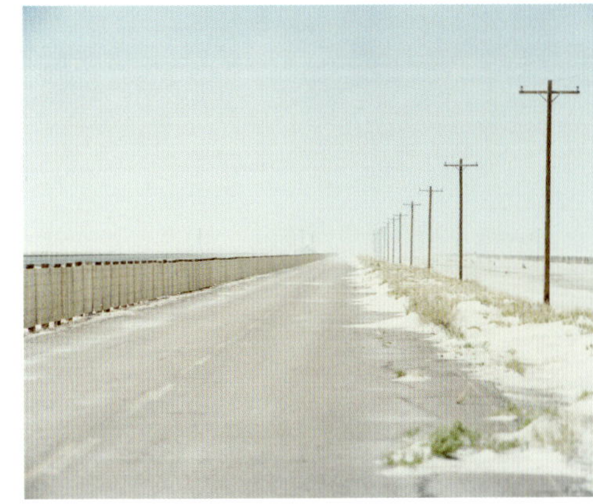

3. Frontage Road II

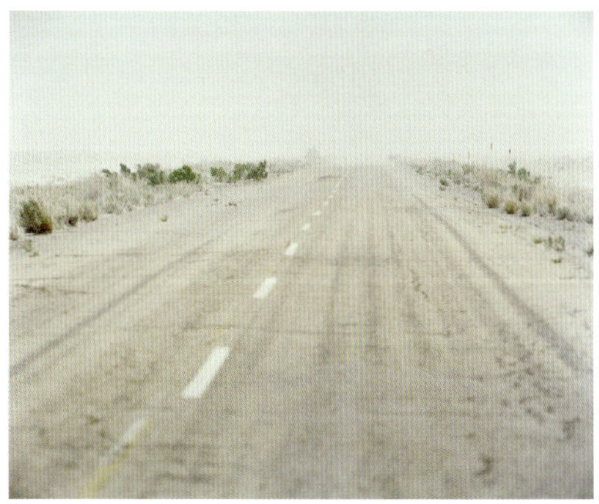

4. Frontage Road III

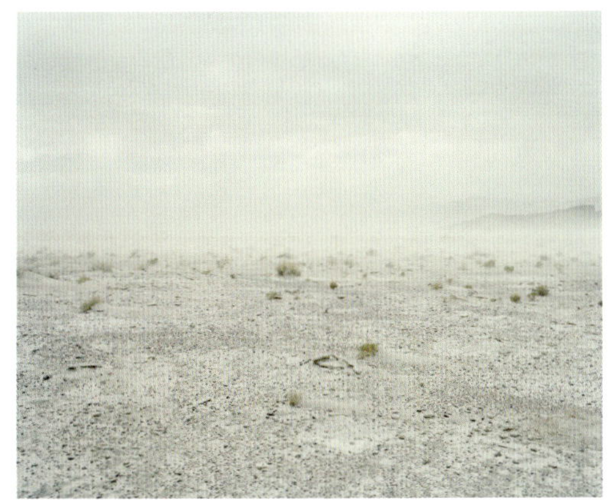

5. Whiteout I

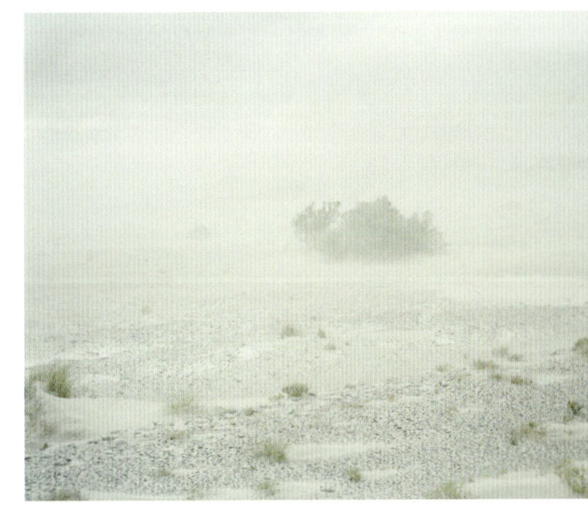

6. Whiteout II

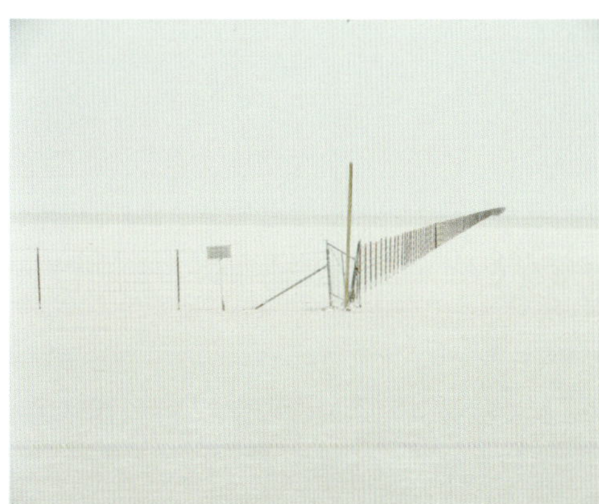

7. Fence-Line Mirage

8. Alkali or Mud

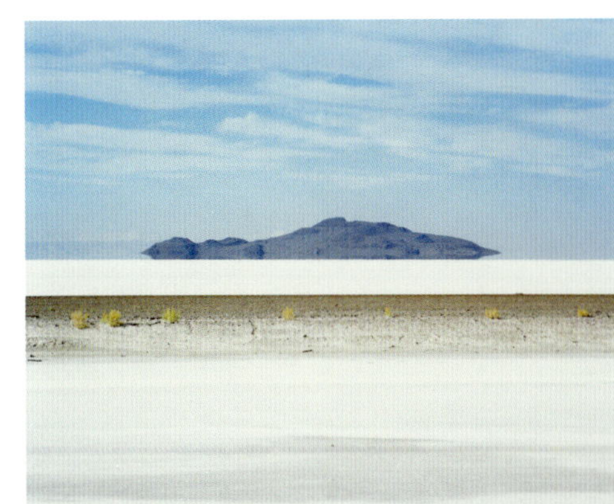

9. Floating Island

II. WENDOVER

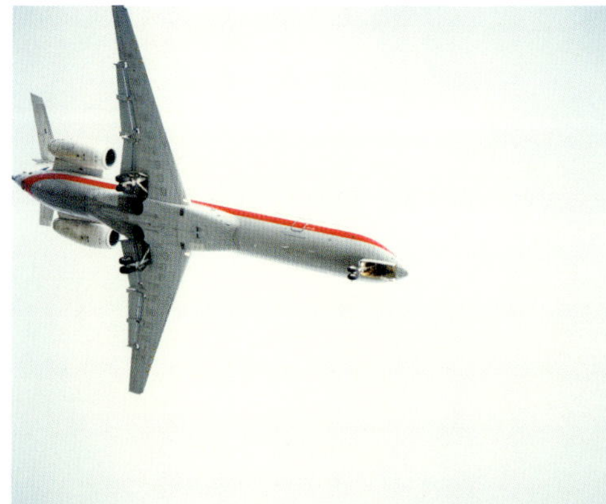

1. Plane with a Red Stripe

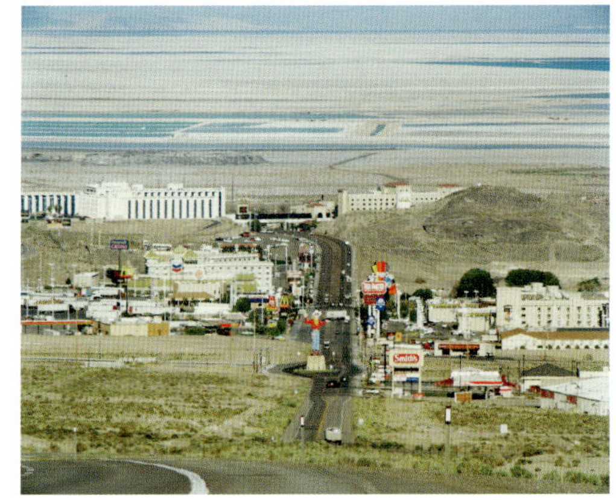

2. View from Interstate 80

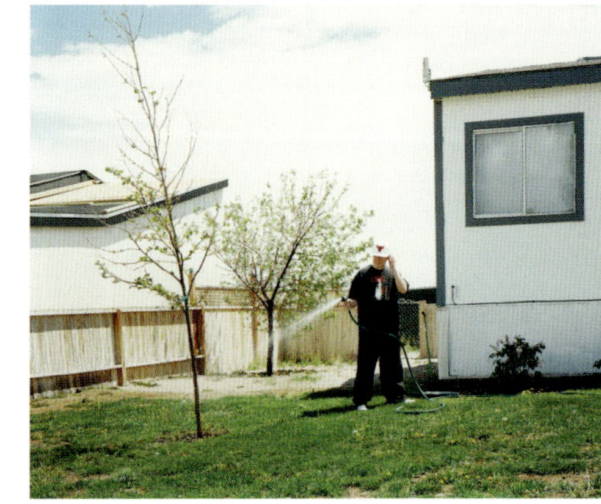

3. Scarface

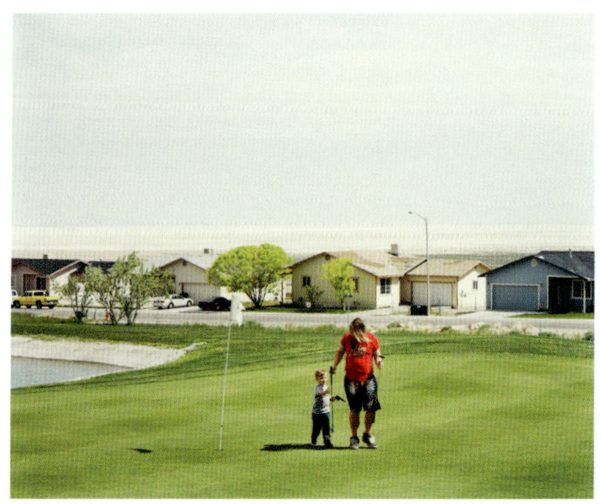

4. Black Sabbath

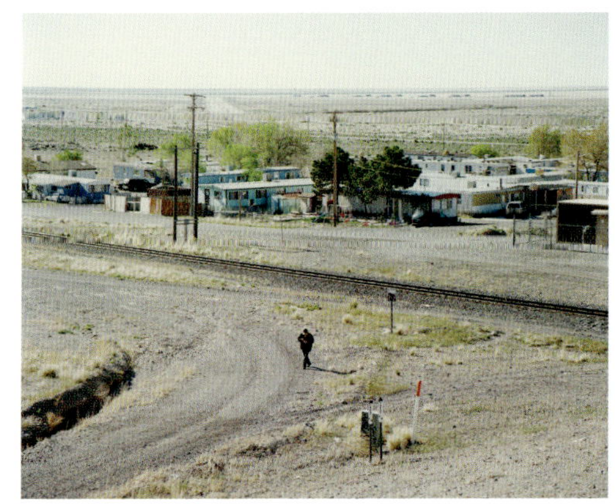

5. Casino Worker

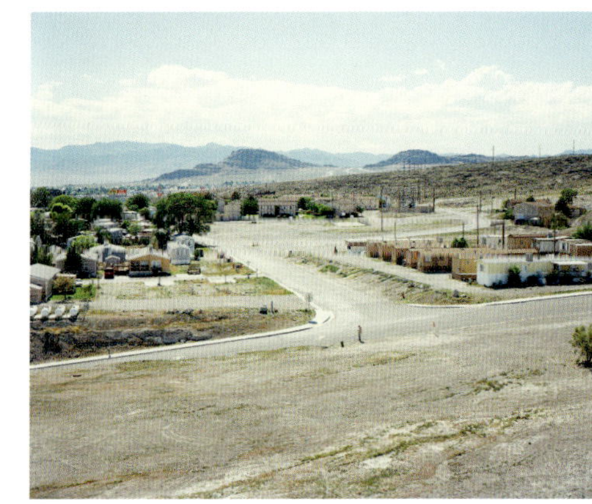

6. Aria Boulevard

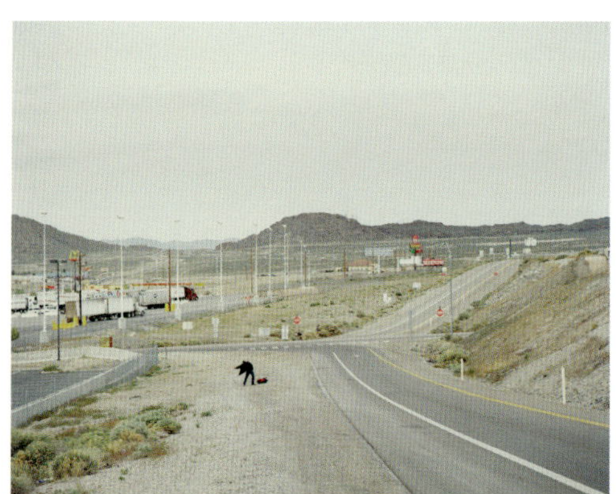

7. Hitchhiker

III. MONTEGO BAY

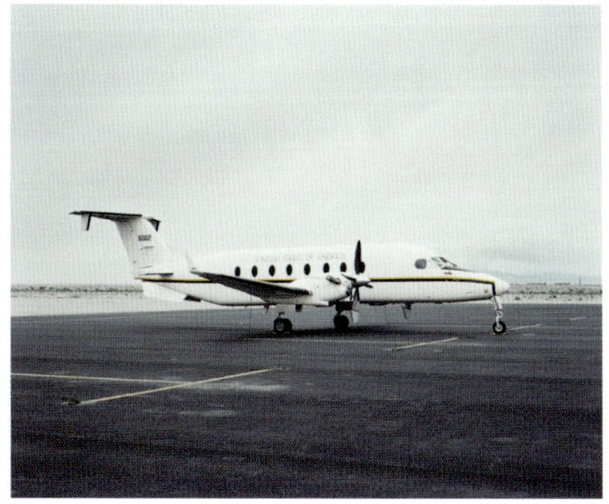

1. United States of America

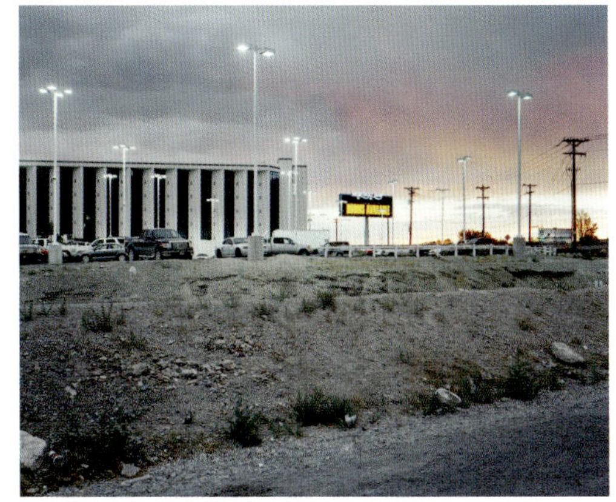

2. Sunset

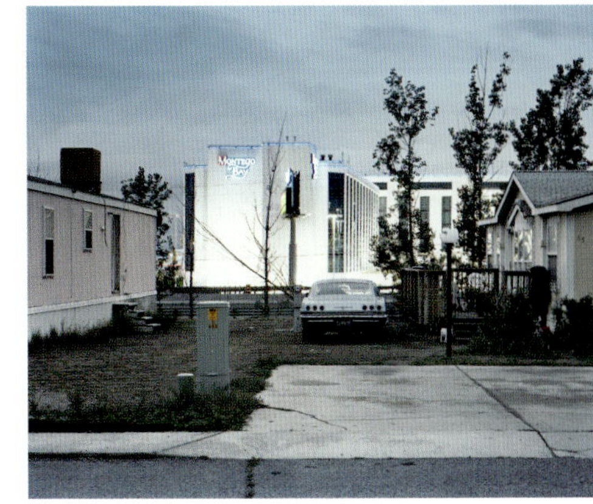

3. Impala

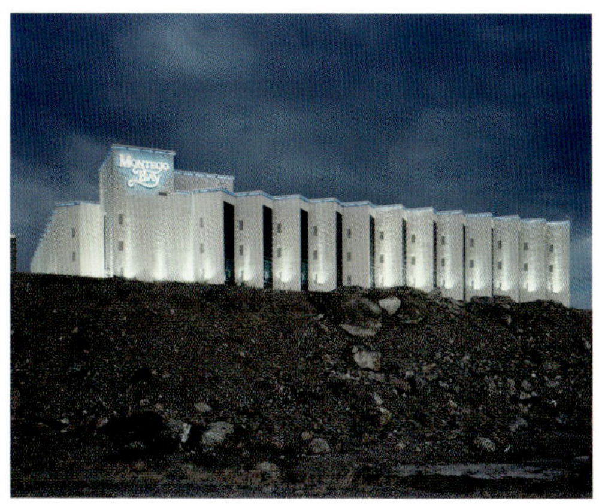

4. Berm

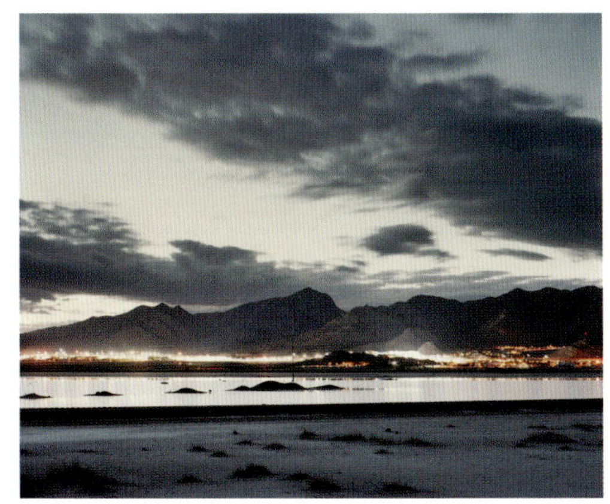

5. View from Southbase

IV. SOUTHBASE

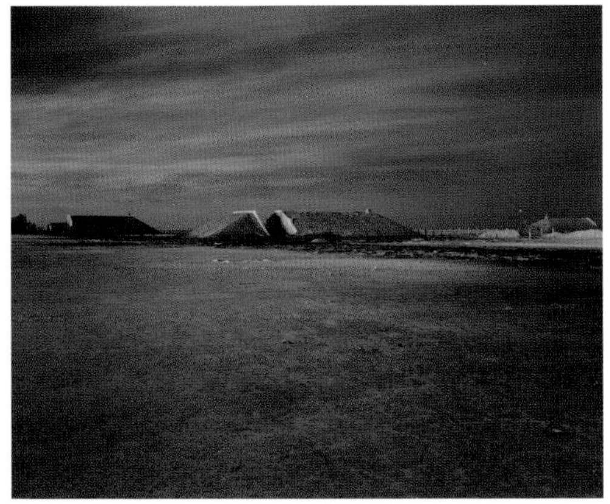

1. Munitions Bunkers

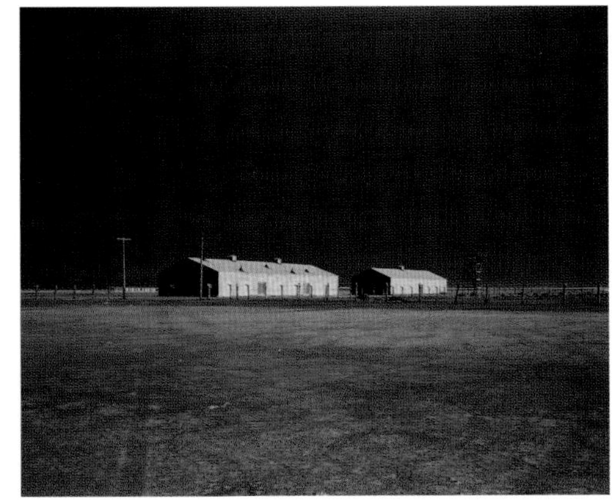

2. Storage Buldings and Movie Tower

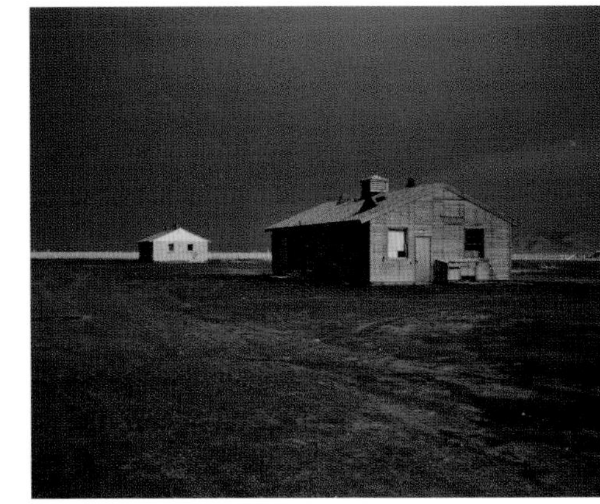

3. Storage Buildings

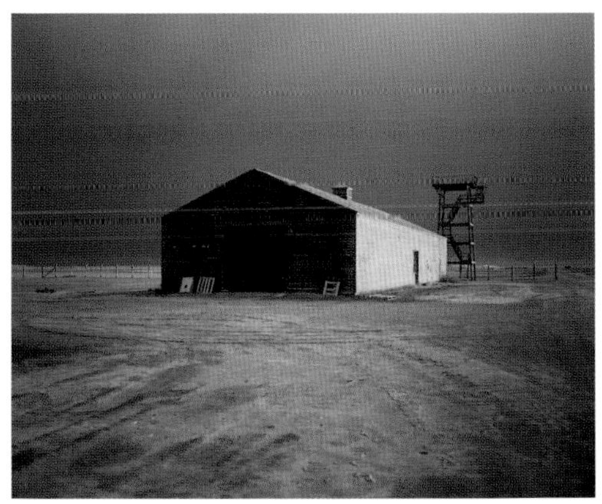

4. Black Hole

5. UTTR

V. UTTR

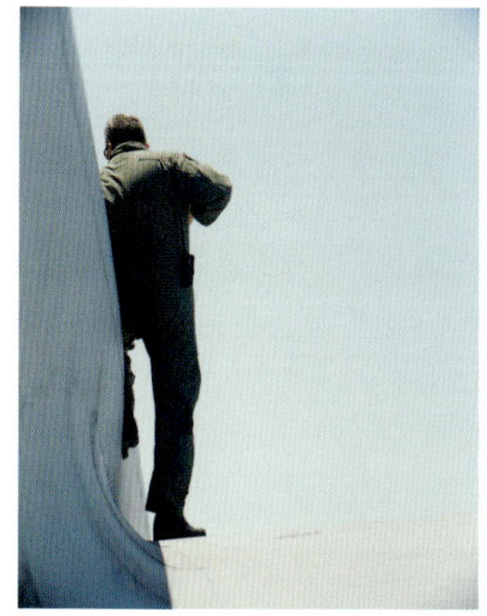

1. Man on the Wing of a KC-135

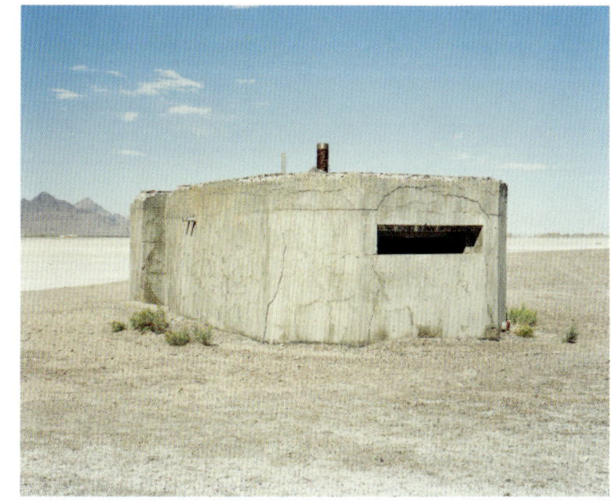

2. Bunker

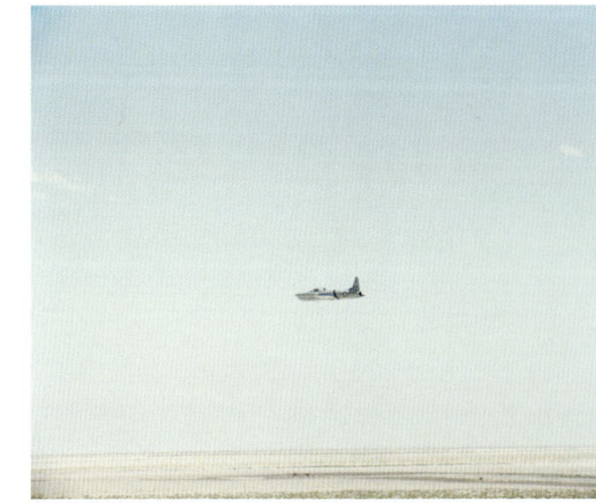

3. T-33

4. Craters

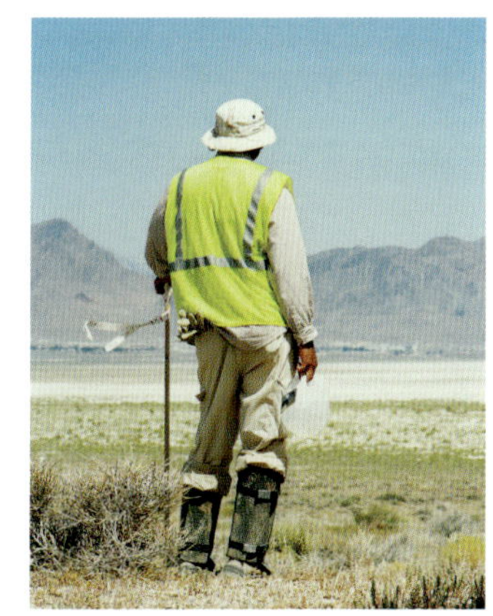

5. Observer

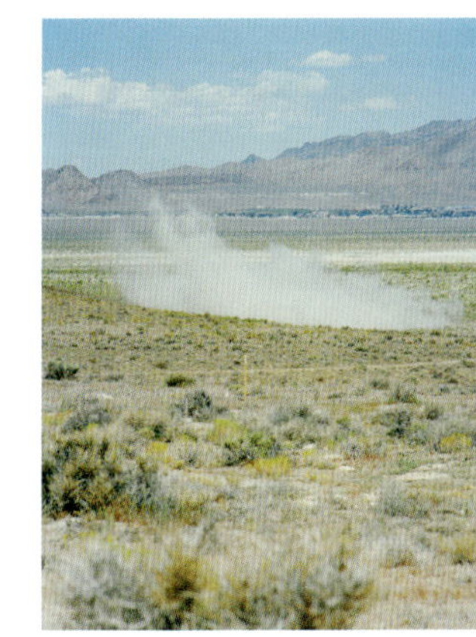

6. Detonation

VI. CASINO

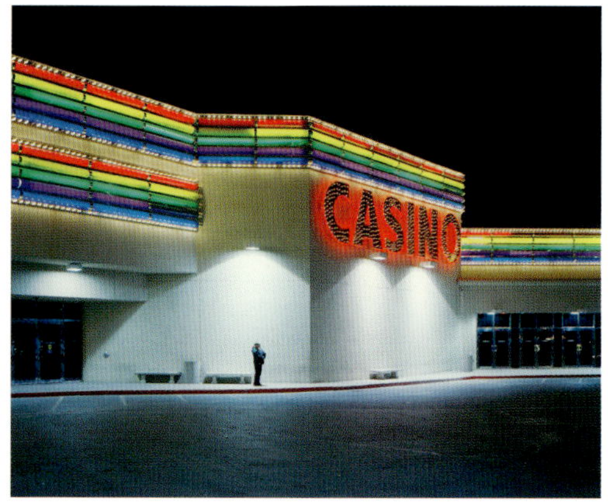

I. Rainbow Casino

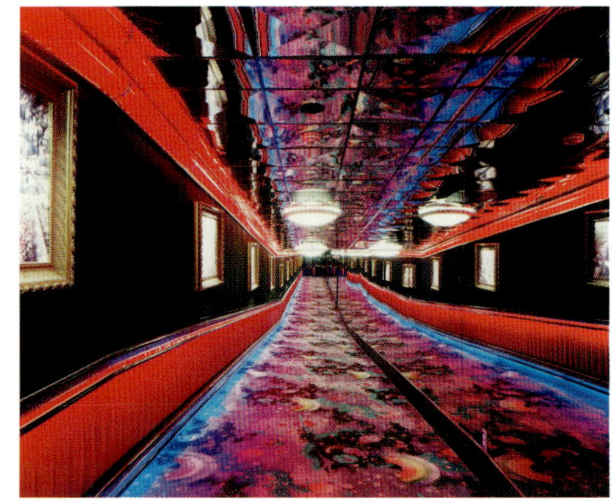

2. Mirrored Hall

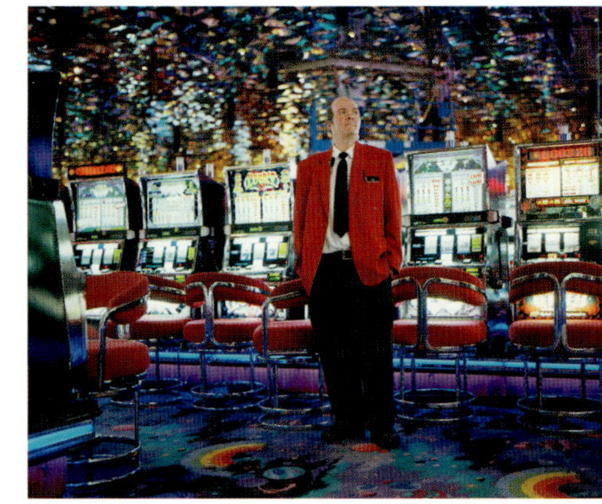

3. Larry, Security

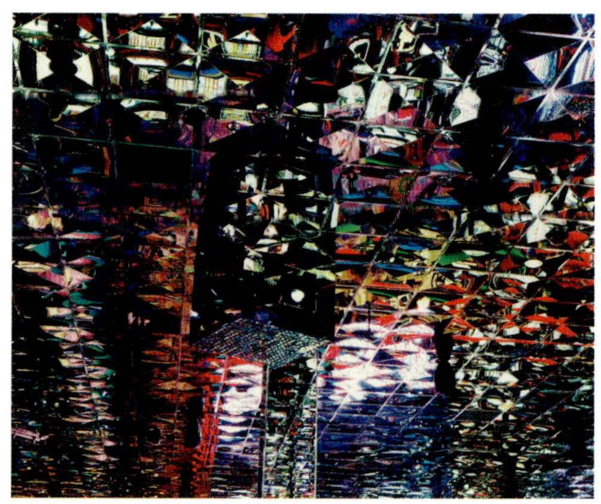

4. Projector

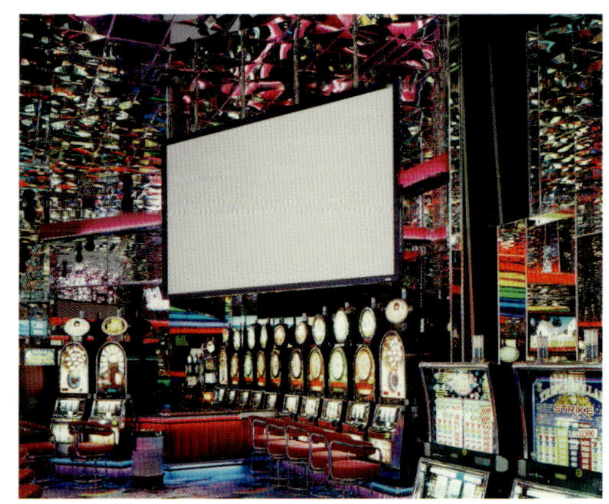

5. Screen

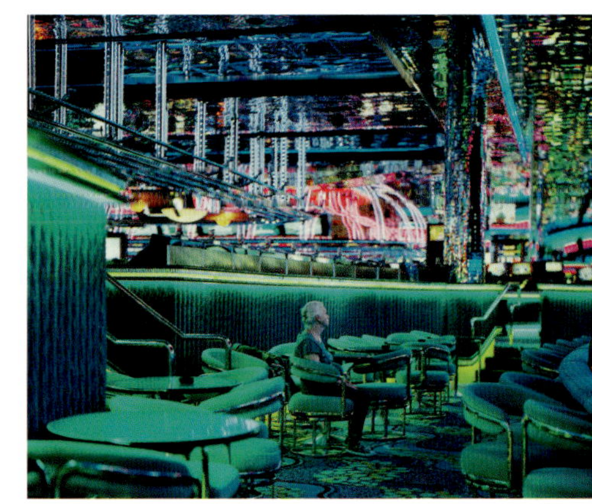

6. Montego Lounge I

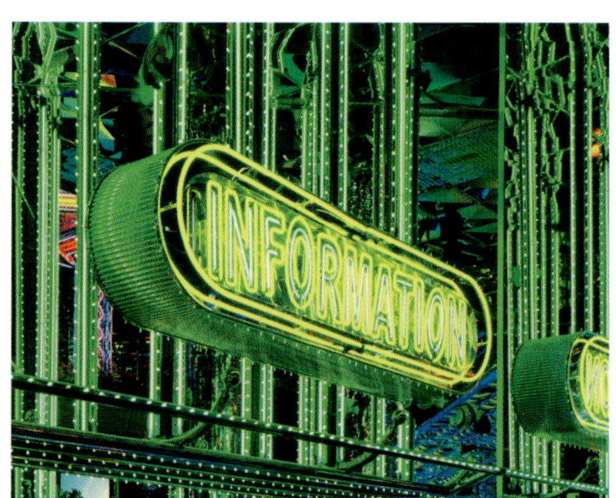

7. Information

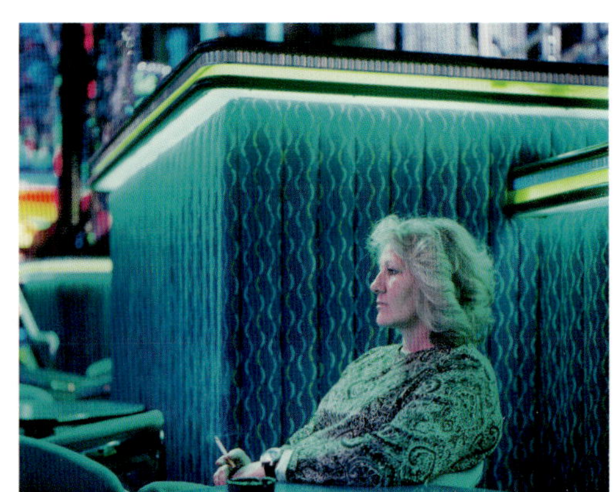

8. Montego Lounge II

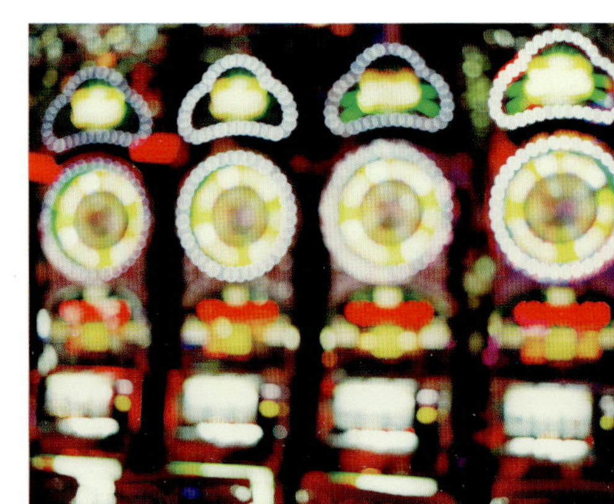

9. Slots

VII. BONNEVILLE

I. Bonneville

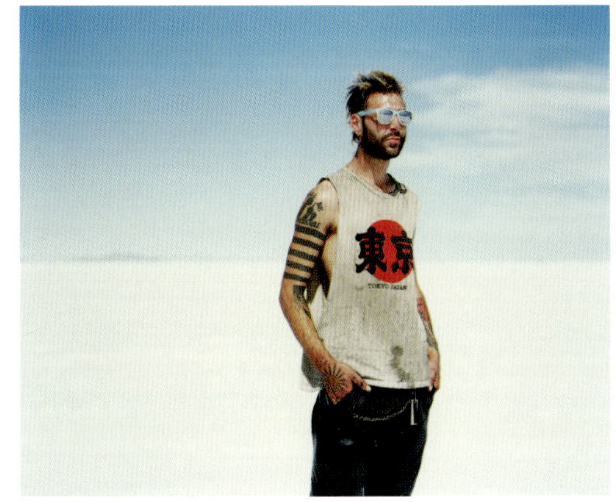

2. Tokyo

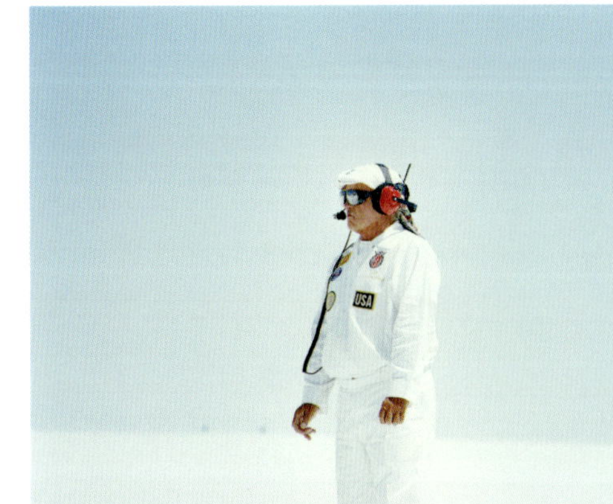

3. USA

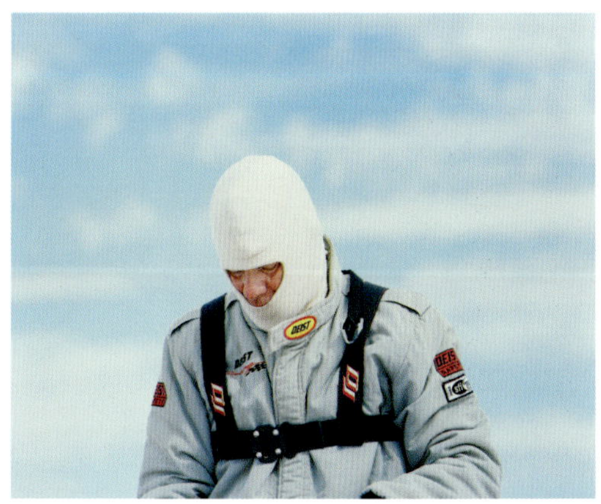

4. Deist

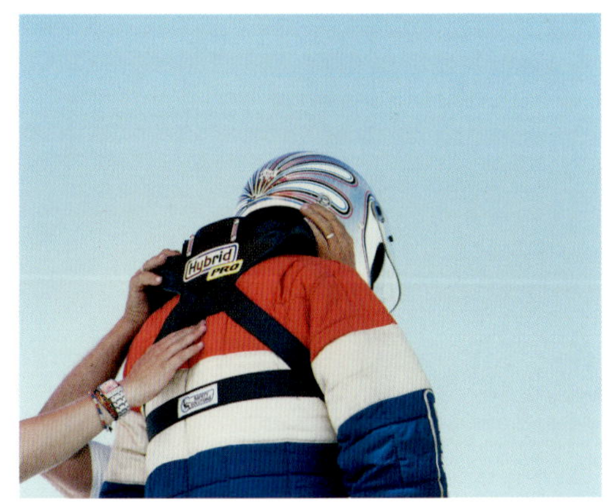

5. Hybrid Pro

VIII. VERTELLUS

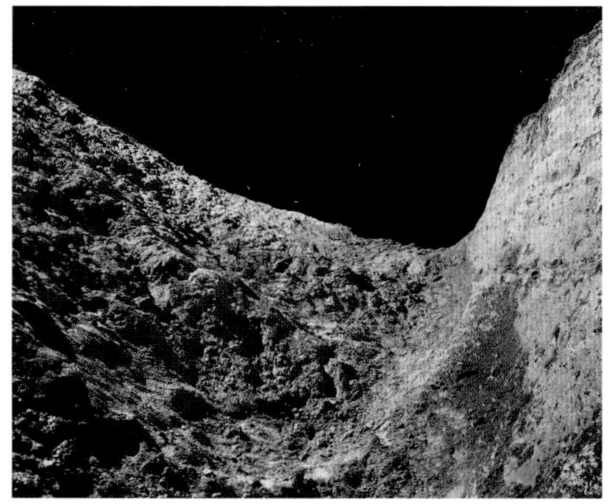

1. Valley I

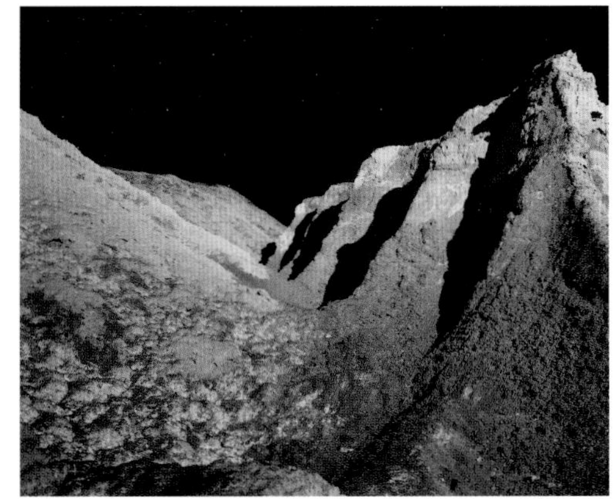

2. Valley II

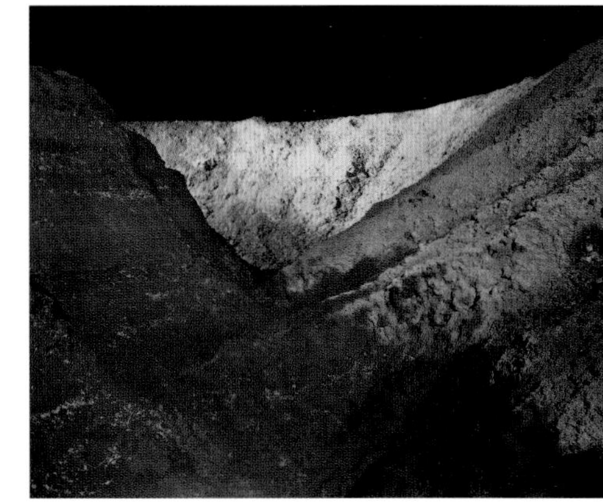

3. Valley III

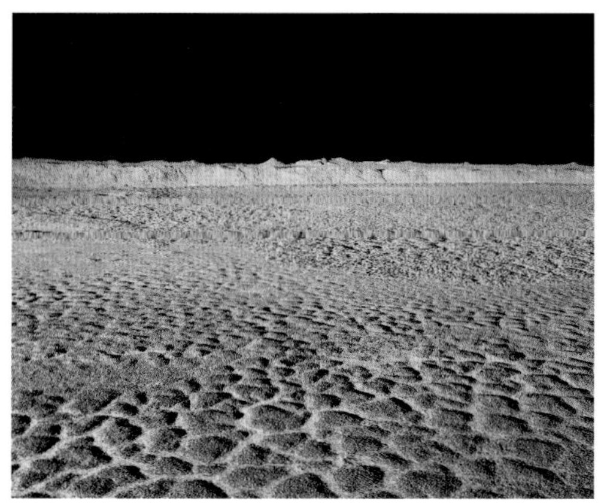

4. Expanse

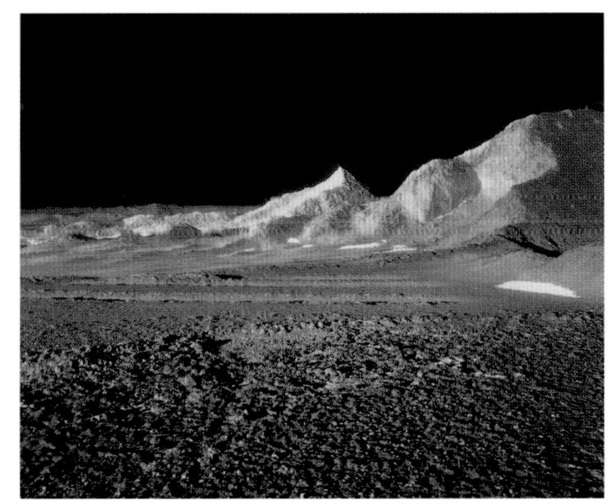

5. Peak

IX. REST AREA

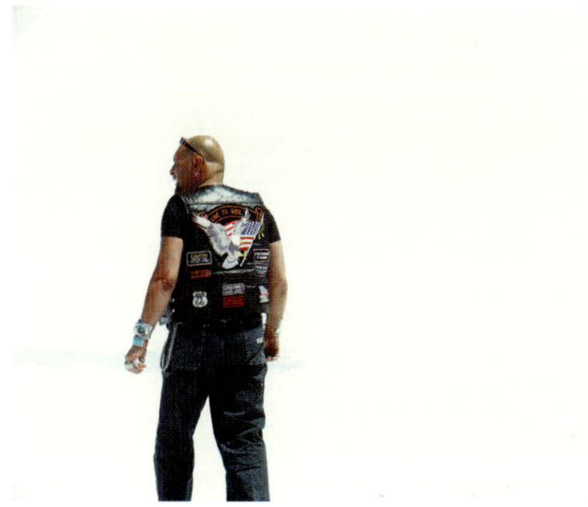

I. Live to Ride

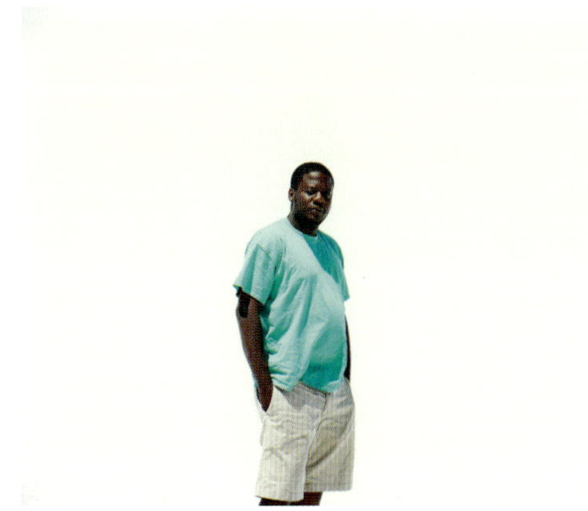

2. Man in a Turquoise Shirt

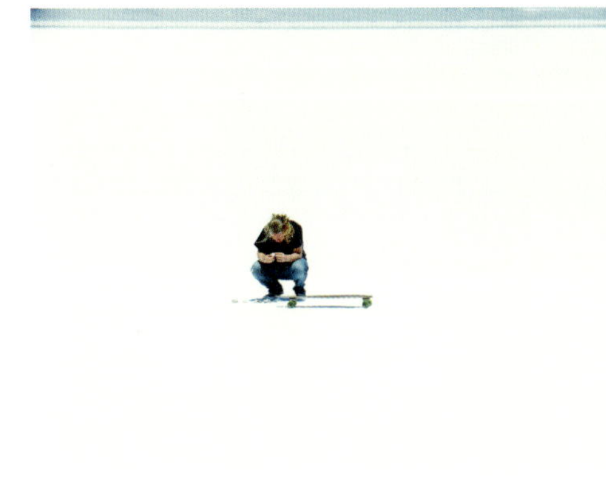

3. Long Board

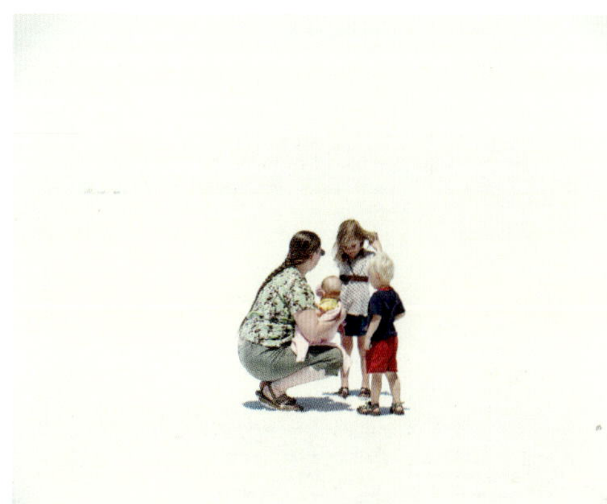

4. Mother and Children

X. NUGGET T748

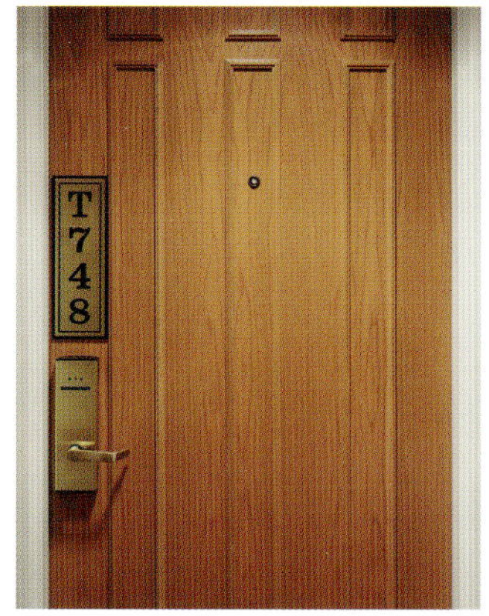

1. T748

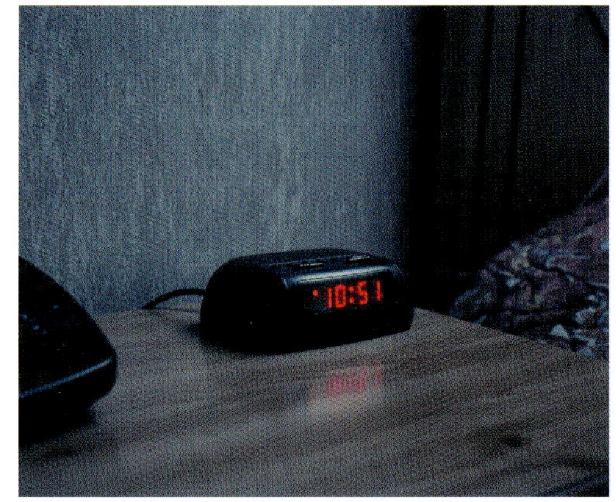

2. 10:51

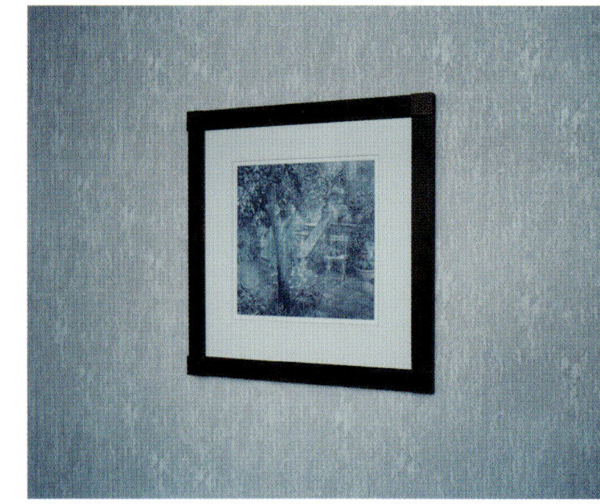
3. Decor

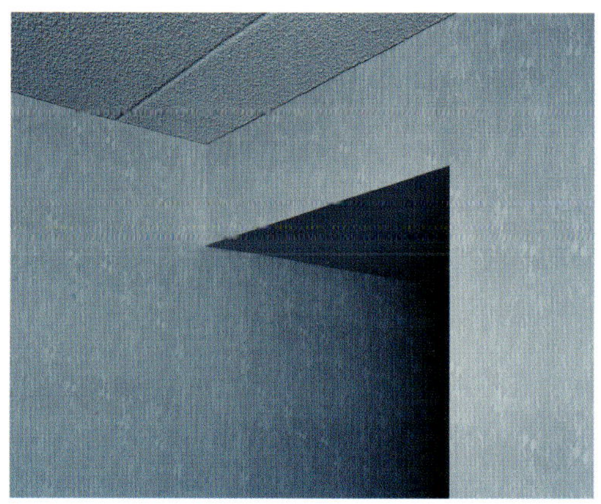
4. Corner

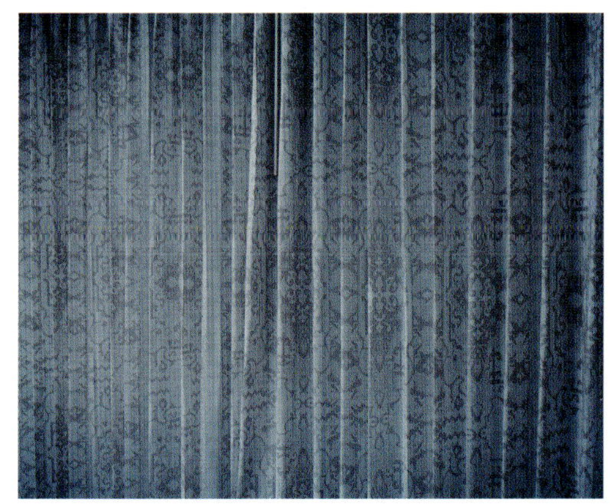
5. Curtain

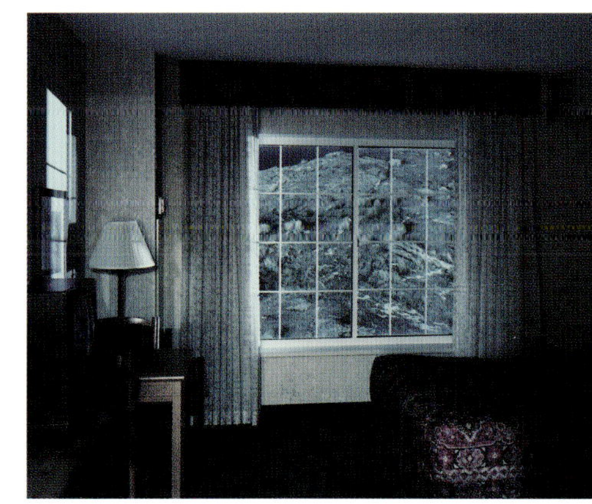
6. Window

ACKNOWLEDGMENTS

For Meggie and Lucas.

Special thanks to Mary Ann Osborne.

The photographs in this book were shot during my time as a participant in the Center for Land Use Interpretation's Wendover Residence Program. Thanks to Matt Coolidge and the CLUI for their vision and generosity.

The book is based on a maquette that was originally commissioned and produced by Artpace San Antonio. For that opportunity, I am grateful to Sarah Lewis and Artpace.

For their generous support of this publication, I extend thanks to Wendy and Mavis Kelsey, Jr., Ann and Tom Kelsey, and Mavis Kelsey III.

I also appreciate the support of Georgetown University and my colleagues in the Department of Art and Art History.

Thanks to Adam Rasmus and Ben Slade of what.it.is creative, my principal collaborators on the book's design. Additional thanks to Ursula Damm for her contribution to the book's design and realization.

For supporting my work in a variety of ways, thanks to Adam Schreiber, Al Acres and Christine Tan, Andy Cherlin and Cynthia Osborne, Anna and Nicholas Brown, Barry Stone, Ben Ruggiero, Bill and Laura Baird, Browne and Diane Goodwin, Caitlin Haskell, Carolina Gutierrez and C. Kent Osborne, Catherine Chao, Chris Evans, Colin Doyle, Eduardo Muñoz Ordoqui, Elizabeth Chiles, Holly Johnson and Jim Martin, Ivete Lucas and Patrick Bresnan, Jessica Mallios, Joan Morgenstern, Joel Leivick, Joey Koehl, John Osborne and Naomi Lopin Osborne, Kim Smith and Michael Hsu, Lawrence McFarland, Mark Goodman, Margie and Mote Baird, Maverick Fisher, Nathan Hensley, Nora Brown and Pete Alrenga, Rick Barot, Ricky Yanas, Rob Ray, Rong Po Chou and Shu Mei Huang, Sarah and Wolfgang Hammer, Teresa Hubbard, Willie Keddell, and Yasufumi Nakamori.

In Wendover, thanks to Chris Melville; Barry Bayorek; Joe Goehring and his colleagues at URS; Corinne and Howard Copelan of the High Desert Advocate; the staff of the Wendover Airport; and the employees of the Montego Bay, Peppermill, Rainbow, Nugget, and Red Garter Casinos.

Finally, thanks to Michael Itkoff and Taj Forer of Daylight Books for believing in the project and bringing it into being.